LILY THE

Stories by

Micky Black

ISBN: 978-1-962886-14-7

Table Of Contents:

Let me start by telling you a little about Lily the Witch 1

LILY THE WITCH AND THE DRAGON CHILD 3

LILY THE WITCH AND WILLOW THE WISP 19

LILY THE WITCH AND THE BOOK OF SHADOWS 36

LILY THE WITCH AND THE BROKEN RAINBOW 51

LILY THE WITCH AND THE FROST KING 65

Let me start by telling you a little about

Lily the Witch

Lily is a good Witch, not the nasty kind. She looks young, and she's tiny, with lovely brown eyes, long dark brown hair - and freckles! She nearly always wears a long cape, and a red jumpsuit. She invents lots of spells, and carries a magic wand (even when she's asleep). With that wand, Lily can do ANYTHING! She has pets – a pair of clever tortoiseshell cats named Honey and Marmalade, and Rags, a lovely little long-haired black and white dog. Like all witches, she keeps a spell book, which she feeds twice a day. Once Rags licked it open while he was playing, spells flew out, and the sky rained frogs until she stopped them!

Lily's home is a cottage on Melody Lane. It's painted red and has a straw roof. Her front garden has flowers which change colour all the time, and a tinkling stream, and behind the cottage there's an orchard with trees which grow oranges, apples and bananas. Now, the cottage itself is peaceful, but be careful, because in its back garden, next to the orchard and hiding under old willow trees, there is a little hill. It's where her elves live - small magical people who help her with spells. All around their hill live huge spiders, and at twilight, or when there's thunder and lightning, the elves come out to play with them and you'll see lots of little shadows running around, ghostly lights, and ghostly music! Scary!

Anyway, getting back to these stories - who's in them? What happens? Well, there's Lily of course, and her elves. Then there's her best friend Bill (he's nice. He's older than Lily and has a beard). Then there's Erzuth the dragon and her family, and of course the Fairies... and say hello to Lily's Shadows. They're copies of Lily (yes, really – when they need to, witches can make copies of themselves! Sometimes they rescue her from danger, too).

Micky Black

Now, every story needs someone wicked, so watch out for Ludo the wizard. Once he was Lily's best friend, they shared magic, and even went flying together (both of them can fly, but only when the sun shines). Sadly, magic made Ludo very greedy, and one day he tried to steal a piece of the Sun. Imagine! But the Sun was too strong and set Ludo on fire, and now he looks a bit like burned toast, and his eyes shine just like the sun. Ever since, he's been trying to put the fires out and be himself again, so he makes lots of mischief, trying to steal magic.

What happens in these Lily the Witch stories? The first one is about a Dragon Child. Dragons have magic, and Ludo stole this one as an egg! Lily's friends the dragons helped save him. The second is when Ludo trapped nearly all the Fairies, and how the very last one saved them with Lily's help. The third is about the Book of Shadows, which traps people and keeps them – but it couldn't keep Lily. In the fourth book Ludo snaps a rainbow in half and tries to poison the world, but Lily, the dragons and the fairies stop him. And the fifth story? It's about how the Frost King (Ludo's wicked brother) tried to freeze the world. Lily said No!

So - enjoy the stories, and look out for more about Lily the Witch

LILY THE WITCH AND THE DRAGON CHILD

One morning, Lily was making breakfast, using a spell from her book of magic. She hadn't tried it before. It was a breakfast spell, all about eggs and bacon. If you spoke the spell forward, it said, (and she did, slowly, just in case) breakfast cooks itself. But never ever say it backward, said the book - or else! So Lily said it the right way, and sure enough there was a blue flash and a squeak, and breakfast was sizzling on the table. Just on the table! 'Bother', she said. 'I forgot the plates!'

So without thinking she tried to undo the spell by saying it backwards. Breakfast vanished, there was an enormous crash, Rags barked and flew out of the door, the cats jumped and flew all the way upstairs, and an enormous pig landed squealing on the kitchen floor. With a plate on its head. Then eggs started falling from the ceiling. Some even landed in her hair. 'Bother!' she said, closing the spell book. The pig vanished, the plate fell on the floor, and as Lily picked it up the eggs all turned into chickens, and went flying out of the window. Rags barked and chased them round the garden!

While Lily was cleaning up, her best friend Bill arrived for breakfast. 'Oh dear', he said. 'Did you drop the spell book again?' 'No' said Lily. 'I just forgot the plates!' Bill scratched his head. 'Forgetting plates makes lots of chickens?' he said. Lily stared. 'What?' she said. 'Take a look', said Bill, pointing out of the window, and when she did it was just in time to see the last chickens flying away. 'That's silly', she said. 'Everyone knows chickens can't fly!' Then there was a fed-up piggy squeal from the ceiling, another blue flash, and... silence. 'Bother', said Lily, sighing. 'I'll have to start breakfast again'.

'Never mind breakfast', said Bill, 'Today's my lucky day – look what I found at the end of your path! Or is it something you've dropped?', and he held out a golden coin, which shone and sparkled as though it was on fire. 'Nice' said Lily. 'But it isn't mine, and I know it wasn't there last night. That's strange. But let's deal with first things first – breakfast! Right now, my tummy's getting fed up.' Bill laughed. 'No - after the spilt food and escaping chickens, your tummy isn't fed up, it's empty' he said. 'And so', he put his hand on his middle, 'is mine. Can we share?' So together they laid the table for breakfast and Lily carefully said that spell again. And after more flashes and a squeak, 'Shhhh bang fizzle squeal!!' lovely hot breakfasts landed on all the plates.

During breakfast they lazily talked about everything from elves to Easter, then once they'd finished Lily stood up with her wand and looked at the plates. 'Shall I help clear up?' said Bill. 'Oh no', Lily replied, smiling, and she tapped the table with her wand, said 'Clean yourself then back on the shelf', and 'Pop!' everything started flying away. 'Lazybones', laughed Bill, holding onto his plate. Then for no obvious reason, he closed his eyes and started rubbing the strange coin, and said 'Nineteen twenty, my plate's empty'. At once there was a bright flash, galloping sounds like angry pigs, lots of 'oink' noises as though the kitchen was filling with pigs, and then plates heaped with bacon and chips and ice cream started fell from the ceiling, and landed in a mess everywhere. Lily stared.

'What did you do!?' she said. Bill looked shocked. Without thinking, he was still rubbing the shining coin with one hand. 'I just said Lazybones', he said, 'and then something like nineteen twenty, my plate's empty'. And before either of them could say another word, more plates full of food were falling from the ceiling and flying in through the door and the windows, and Lily had to wave her wand and shout 'Go home, leave us alone!' before the table and everywhere else became covered with breakfast and ice cream! 'Don't repeat it, we can't eat it', she said. 'Send it back where it belongs!' and the kitchen immediately filled with strong farmyard smells. Lily, Bill and Rags had to run outside as fast as they could, to escape!

As they ran, Lily snatched the coin from Bill. 'Let me see that' she said. They ran into the orchard behind Lily's cottage and stayed there for a long while to let the farmyard smells go. Lily kept turning the coin over and over in her hands, until her fingers were twitching and tingling. 'I've got a bad feeling about this coin' she said, closing her eyes. 'I know where it came from and what it does', and she frowned. 'It's Ludo's - he's out to make more trouble, and for some reason he wants that trouble to start here! I need to talk with my elves! Please stay here with Rags, and look after my cottage', she said. 'Oh, and don't let anybody in', and she walked quickly across the garden to the elves' little hill under the willow trees, knocked politely on the door, and went inside.

Quickly, the elves gathered round, smiling, and all of them started talking. She waved a hand in the air (being very careful not to wave the shining coin) and said 'Hi everyone. Can you just shush for a minute? I need to talk with the Head Elf'. Quickly, he appeared and pushed his way through the crowd. He reached out to give Lily a hug - but then stopped and sniffed (elves can smell magic!) 'Ludo!'he said, and Lily nodded, showing him the coin. 'Bill found this outside my cottage this morning. Yes, it's Ludo's, he throws them to make his magic stronger and stop other people's spells.' 'It smells horribly powerful!' said the Head Elf. 'It is!' said Lily. 'Bill found it, then at breakfast he waved it and it filled my kitchen with a billion breakfasts and horribly strong farmyard smells! I wonder what Ludo's up to.' and as she spoke there was an enormous bang from outside. They rushed to see what had happened. There were clouds of grey, smelly smoke everywhere, the grass had been scorched as though by a fire, but worst of all, her cottage door was open and scorched black, there was no sign of Bill or of Rags, and a dragon was just disappearing over the trees!

They held their noses and ran to the cottage. Honey and Marmalade, Lily's cats, flew down from an upstairs window, their fur standing on end. 'What happened?' said Lily. 'Where is everyone?' They looked at her, their eyes wide, and said 'Just after you went into the elves' home, a hot shadow flew over the cottage. That shadow looked like Ludo. He was carrying something big and shiny, and then a huge dragon caught up with him and blew flames at him. He screamed and dropped what he'd been carrying with a big bang, and then flew off ever so fast, with the dragon still chasing him and blowing flames. There was lots of fire and smoke. We think Bill and Rags ran to your cellar!' said Marmalade. And they had – they looked carefully around before coming out, then they both helped tidy up the mess.

'So why did he leave that coin by your path?' said Bill. 'I've been thinking about that', said Lily the Witch. 'I think it was to distract me, so that I didn't know what he was doing. Coins like that are powerful, they're very good at hiding spells except for the person who made them, so this was made to stop me using magic! They only work once, so this one wilbe no good, but I wonder what Ludo was carrying?' said Lily, and at once a deep dark voice spoke in her mind. 'Greetings, little mother! It is me, your dragon friend Erzuth. He has stolen a dragon egg, so I chased him and burned him, but he can fly much faster than me, and he has dropped it somewhere! I must find it!' Now, when Lily gets very cross, she stomps around the trees in her orchard, because that calms her down. And she was very cross. She mind-spoke 'Erzuth, He is wicked. We will help you search! He has damaged my cottage too and I'm very cross!'

She walked through the orchard with Bill. The orchard held lots and lots of magical trees. Maybe today you'll find apples, but then tomorrow you'll find oranges. Or even bananas. Because there were so many trees you couldn't see from one side of the orchard to the other, but sadly they soon found a trail of tree stumps, leading to the furthest corner of the orchard.

Lily was cross about that too and mended all the damaged trees quickly. And when she'd finished, right in the corner of the orchard, that's when they had to stop and stare - because under the very last tree, sleeping in the warm sunshine, was a great big shiny white egg! 'It's beautiful!' said Bill. 'No chicken ever laid an egg like it. Not even a crocodile could!'Lily smiled, her anger quite forgotten. It's a dragon's egg' she said. Bill's eyes widened and he quickly looked around. 'So somewhere nearby there may be dragons? Hadn't we better hide?' 'We don't need to, my friend', she said. 'I'm sure this egg belongs to my dragon friend Erzuth. You're safe, but we must hide the egg from Ludo. I think Erzuth burned him and he had to drop it, then it rolled here.It's been through a lot, but there isn't even one mark on it.' 'Dragon eggs must be really tough!' said Bill. 'Yes', said Lily, 'they are. And the Dragon Child inside is very tough too.' 'So how do we protect it? said Bill. 'In my kitchen', said Lily the Witch. They walked quickly back to the kitchen, and Lily made a spell to bring the egg indoors and put it safely in a blanket under her breakfast table. They hid it just in time! Danger! There was a bright flash, birds stopped singing, the sun burned hot enough to cook dinner, and something laughing, dark and nasty flew low across the garden, dropping lots of sparkly things wherever he went ('He's throwing sunspots to look for the egg. Shh!'). But of course the Dragon Child's egg was nowhere to be found, and Ludo eventually flew away, the sunspots fizzled out, and everything went back to normal - the birds sang, the apples in the orchard turned into pineapples, and the cottage was peaceful once again.

The friends hugged each other and smiled. 'We did it!' said Bill, looking proudly at the egg, which was still and beautiful under the kitchen table, with Lily's cats Honey and Marmalade keeping it warm. They thought about what to do next. 'There's only one thing to do', said Lily. 'I must tell Erzuth. She can come and fetch the Dragon Child back to her mountain before Ludo tries tearing my cottage apart looking for it!' But try as she may, Lily couldn't mind-speak Erzuth. 'She's not answering me' she said. 'That egg needs to go home quickly, so it looks as though we'll have to make an expedition to Dragonmount, and tell her, because moving the egg all that way would be too hard even for strong magic like mine!'

'Good, said Bill. 'Let's have an expedition!' 'Well, that won't be easy', said Lily, 'You see, dragons can be invisible until you trip over them!’ Bill looked amazed. 'The thing about dragons', she said, explaining, 'is that they know how to disappear. One moment you see them, the next moment they’re not there’. Bill stared. ‘What, just like a magician drops rabbits into a hat?' he said. Lily scratched her head. ‘Well, nearly’, she said. ‘But dragons don’t really disappear, they’re still there, you just can’t see them’. Bill looked confused. ‘It’s because of how they use colours’, said Lily. ‘Dragons are a bit like those funny lizardy things called chameleons. If they keep still, they can be the same colour as whatever they’re resting on. And that makes things even worse – they’re so big you can just walk right into them!’ Bill sat and thought for a moment. ‘So finding your friend Erzuth may be a problem?' 'It all depends whether she wants to be seen', said Lily. ‘I shall keep trying to mind-speak and ask her.’ But Erzuth still wasn’t answering.

After lunch, they couldn’t resist looking again under the table at the egg. It was big, calm and beautiful, and Lily got on her knees to listen to it, but there was nothing to hear. ‘I don’t think the Dragon Child is ready to hatch yet’, she said, regaining her feet. Bill raised an eyebrow. 'That's good - it means we have some time to find its mother', she said, turning to her cats. 'But if we’re going on an expedition, I’ll need you two cats to snuggle up to the egg and keep it warm and comfortable? And if anything happens, you know how to talk with me when I'm somewhere else'. 'What? How...?' said Bill.

‘It's difficult to explain’, she said. ‘My cats, Rags and I talk in my head, and I can talk back with them. I call it mind-speak. Rags and my cats are very special! You should learn to do it, Bill!. The cats purred, Rags wagged his tail, and the friends decided they’d start the next day. In the morning, Bill tapped on the door just as Lily was finishing her breakfast, and they both smiled and said ‘Hello’ at the same time. ‘No coins by your path today’, said Bill. ‘Are you ready for our visit to the dragons?’ ‘Yes, nearly ready’, said Lily, 'There are just a few things I need to pack. Won’t be long'. Bill nodded, and as she packed, Lily told him what she would be taking. There were some very odd things, too! A mirror (‘because sometimes you can see dragon reflections in a mirror, even when you can't see dragons', she said); an apple pie made with apples from her orchard ('dragon mother as present – dragons think that's good manners'). 'Apple pie?' said Bill. 'Yes', she said. 'They love apples'.

The next thing she packed was custard powder. 'Custard powder?' said Bill, 'Whatever's that for?' 'Well', said Lily, 'If you think maybe there's a dragon in front of you, you blow some of this in the air, and when it settles not only can you see the dragon, but it is so busy licking up custard powder it doesn't stop to breathe fire at you!' Bill laughed. 'Custard powder!' he said. 'You think of everything!' 'I've had lots of adventures with dragons', she said. 'I told you about Erzuth, She's one of the biggest of them all, and one of my best friends, and she has always loved custard, with or without apples! I did go and talk with the elves, but they said they hadn't been able to mind-speak any of the dragons and didn't know where they might be! So I think Erzuth's just keeping quiet until she's decided what to do'.

They finished packing food and all the things Lily the Witch thought they might need, into two large wicker baskets. 'How are we going to carry those up a mountain?' said Bill. Lily laughed. 'Simple', she said. She clapped her hands, and the baskets grew wings and jumped into the air all by themselves. 'Now, Rags', said Lily, 'you may come with us, but behave. I don't want to see you getting squashed or cooked alive!' The little dog sat down and cocked her head. Lily the Witch laughed. 'No, not really', she said. 'But you do have to behave. And you cats', she added, turning to Honey and Marmalade, 'Please keep my cottage safe, and mind-speak me if anything happens to that egg. Eat any sunspots that try to get in! Now, I'm just going to tell the elves what we're doing!'

She went up her garden and knocked 'tap a tap tap' on the green door. It was locked – the elves were taking no chances! They peeked out to see who it was, and unlocked the door and let her in, then quickly crowded around to hear what she had to say. It was no surprise that they already knew about the egg. 'We knew something was happening', said the Head Elf. 'We'd seen smoke on that mountain you call Dragonmount, and we saw a dragon rise into the sky and start chasing something. Then when it got closer, we saw it was Ludo, flying very low and carrying something big and white! Well, we thought it had to be mischief, but we didn't want to get in the way so we stayed here – and you know the rest!'

'Yes, we found the egg while we were in the orchard', said Lily the Witch. 'I thought it must be Ludo's doing - he always steals things which might be useful and dragon eggs are very magical, so I'm sure he will come looking for it again. If he does, use your spells to send him away! Bill and I are going with Rags right now to find and talk with Erzuth. I will mind-speak with you once we know what's happening, and there are two things I'll need you to be ready to do: make the sky black so he can't fly, and then make him very wet. He hates that.   I don't care how you do it, she said, but be ready! And then amid lots of cheering, singing and stamping of feet, (excited elves always stamp their feet) she left to start the adventure - Lily and Bill, with Rags dancing and sometimes flying alongside and the baskets flying too.

Lily led the way, with her wand firmly grasped in her hand. 'Let's start off by going over the old stone bridge and then up into the hills, and on to the mountains', she said. 'I'm sure we will find dragons up there, even if my elves can't speak with them yet.' So they walked patiently along Melody Lane until they reached the bridge and the crossroads, where signs pointed toward the Mountains, the villages, and the Cottage of Lily the Witch.

Bill turned and waved. 'See you soon, my little village!' he said. And they walked beside the little stream, along the stony path toward the hills, the sleeping trees, and the mountains, and left Melody Lane and Lily's thatched cottage far behind. She pointed to the stream - 'I don't think we'll find dragons near any water. They worry in case it puts out their flames! They don't much like trees either, they make it difficult to land and take off. But on the mountains, they have all the room they need'.

All morning they climbed through the woods, stopping every now and then for a rest. Rags the little dog didn't seem to need rests - he sniffed everything he could find, then jumped and barked when he was surprised by squirrels. 'Shh!', said Lily. 'We don't want anyone to know we're here. Not even dragons, unless we know they're friendly like Erzuth! Try to stay quiet until we know we've found the dragon mother', and she waved her wand, to calm Rags.

The trees grew further apart as they climbed higher, until they could see the rolling green hills and the purply-grey mountains beyond. 'Nearly there' said Lily. 'It's a long time since I was up here, and coming back makes me happy'. She gave Bill a quick hug and he smiled and said 'I remember coming up here with you once, and seeing hedgehogs and rabbits, birds and butterflies eating out of your hand'. 'Because I was happy', she said. 'It's so unspoilt here, just as it should be everywhere. I love it and I do my best to care for it.

Once they reached the hills, the sky seemed to go on forever, above the looming mountains, with just a little cotton wool cloud here and there. But of dragons there was no sign. Lily the Witch took out her mirror and used it to look around, but there were no dragons even in the mirror. She mind-spoke with the cats at her cottage, but everything was peaceful there, too (although what the cats didn't say was that they'd started talking with the Dragon Child). But from Erzuth there was silence. At last, they reached a rocky place which gave them all room to sit down, and places for Rags to explore. They caught the two flying baskets, unwrapped their lunch (some of Lily's apple pie, and some fruit and vegetables) and started eating as though they were in a race. Which quickly (and without warning), they were.

Suddenly, the sun sent a scorching hot wind, and Lily looked sharply around. 'That's Ludo', she said, and waved her wand around them. Instantly, they were covered in mist. 'There, he cannot see us now', she said, 'but we must be quiet! Rags, where are you?' The little dog ran out from behind a large rock and jumped into her arms. 'Quiet now', she said, and they heard a sparky, crackling noise, and felt the heat grow further and then fade as Ludo flew past. 'I wonder why he's come back up here. Maybe to see if there's another dragon egg, or to make some other mischief. I just wish we could warn the dragons. But I can't.' And then just as she spoke, the Dragon Child mind-spoke his mother. 'I'm safe, mother, in Lily's cottage with Honey and Marmalade, but someone called Ludo is out to find you!'

Very soon after, as Lily's mist cleared, they watched a huge green dragon fly into the sky over the mountains, breathing fire and smoke, and chasing after a sparkly black shape, which flew quickly away. 'Look', said Leo. 'That's amazing!' Lily turned to see, and a bright smile lit her face. 'That's my old friend Erzuth! Wonderful! Fly on, my friend!' But having chased Ludo from the mountains, the dragon quickly settled back on the ground and vanished from sight. She sighed. 'At least we know there are dragons on Dragonmount! Let's start our search there'.

They quickly tidied their lunch away, and carried on walking among the hills and toward the mountains. The sky was bright and clean all around them, the air was fresh and sweet, and all three of them – Lily the Witch, Bill and Rags - loved feeling so free. They passed wooded valleys, rocky streams, groups of rabbits playing in the sun, some sheep and some goats, and then they were approaching Dragonmount itself. 'I can't see any dragons yet', said Bill. 'Maybe not, but keep looking', said Lily. 'The higher we go, the better'. So they carried on climbing towards the top. Rags skipped around, keeping a watchful eye open for squirrels, and chasing them everywhere. He barked and chased one up a particularly high and slippery mound - and then stopped in surprise! The top of the mound moved, a great big eye opened. and it felt as though the whole mountain shook itself slightly before a deep voice rumbled from a rocky hollow. 'Lily Witch! Is that you? Walking up my back?! It is me, your friend Erzuth'. And part of the rich green hillside simply stood up. Rags fell roly-poly off the mound and shook himself, stared at this new arrival, then ran!

Bill sat down with a bump, too. 'Goodness', he said. 'That's not mountain – it's dragon! We don't even need custard powder!' Lily smiled. 'Erzuth', she said, with a very happy look on her face. And then everyone started mind-speaking (Bill had learned how to do it on the way to the mountain, Lily and Erzuth were talking about the missing Dragon Child, and several other dragons were joining in too. And all this time Rags was still running down the mountain with his tail between his legs... Eventually, the talking got too loud. Lily threw her head back and laughed, then mind-shouted 'Stop! Stop! Stop!' Both Bill and Lily shook their heads and rubbed their ears. 'That was loud!' said Bill.

'Yes, it was a bit silly', said Lily, 'but it's wonderful to find Erzuth again, although it's been sad too. Honey, Marmalade, what is happening? I can hear another voice. Is that our egg?' When the cats said yes, it was, Lily and the dragons all welcomed the Dragon Child, then said they would explain everything. But before she did, Lily wanted to find Rags, who was by now a long way down the mountain! 'Find him? Leave this to me', said Erzuth.

Now, if you have ever seen a dragon start flying, you know what a wonderful sight it can be. And Erzuth was an enormous dragon. Her wings spread so far the sky was almost hidden! She flapped them slowly and powerfully and she flew straight up into the air before gliding silently down towards Rags. When she caught up with the little dog, she mind-spoke and said 'Stop, I wish you no harm, I am your friend. Please come back with me so we can all be together'. Rags stopped and looked shyly at Erzuth, before starting to wag his tail, then the dragon picked him up and flew back to Lily.

'Now', said Lily, once they were all together again, 'Erzuth, my heart is happy seeing you - it has been far too long. And I wish we had met again in happier times, but at least we have met. Let me tell you why we're here', and she talked to all the dragons about what the elves had seen, about Ludo being near her cottage and burning it, about finding the dragon's egg, and about Ludo flying over them on their way up the mountain. 'You really frightened him' she said to

Erzuth. 'Yes, little mother', said Erzuth, but he will return. He still wants an egg!'

'We have struggled with Ludo before', said Lily. Trying to steal some of the sun's magic really changed him. I'm sad and angry that he managed to steal the egg.' 'Yes,' said Erzuth, 'That belongs to a young dragon who lives with me' 'Thankyou so much for travelling to find us' rumbled a new voice, as another big green dragon appeared from nowhere, rising up from the mountainside. 'I am Rezu. Ludo must have sneaked up on me while I was asleep. I was keeping three eggs warm, and the one he stole must have wobbled free - it made me very worried, although Erzuth did tell me all about you. She said you would help me find him, and he would be safe near you, little mother. And he is. Thankyou so much!'

As Rezu sat up (she was nearly as big as Erzuth), Lily hugged Rags so he felt safe, and Bill jumped backwards at the sight of another dragon. 'And are your other two children safe?' said Lily, and two little green dragons no bigger than Rags, poked their heads around their mother's wings. 'Yesss little mother', they said.

They all thought about what to do next. They were using mind-speak, and Bill smiled as he joined in. 'It's good to mind-speak everyone', she said, 'But from this moment, while we're deciding what to do, and until we're ready, we should really just talk, because if Ludo hears us mind-speaking, he'll know what we plan to do', said Erzuth, and very soon Lily the Witch, Bill, Erzuth and Rezu and her two babies had agreed a plan. Rezu would mind-speak 'Help me, I'm lost!' in a high-pitched voice, as loudly as she could, so that Ludo could hear, and would come to see what new nastiness he could do.

When he arrived they would tempt him with a great big stone the size, shape and colour of a dragon's egg, leaving it where it could easily be seen, and close to where the dragons slept. The dragons and the babies would hide themselves like before ('That was so clever!' said Bill), and once Ludo came to see what the noise was about and think how lucky he was to find another egg, they would spring the surprise and hold him down on the hillside, so Lily could spellbind him. 'It's no use just telling him not to do these things', said Bill. 'Someone needs to prevent him from flying!' 'Now that is a very good idea', said Erzuth. 'But it's probably easier said than done - he is strong and VERY sneaky! Let's all think about it.'

First, Rezu flew down Dragonmount to where there were many boulders, and within a few minutes she returned with a big one in her claws that was just like an egg. 'That looks perfect', said Lily. 'Let's find the right spot for it', and Rezu and Erzuth looked around and found a shallow grassy hollow on the hillside. 'Here, here will be fine, it's not far from where my egg must have been stolen', said Rezu. 'And there will be plenty of room for us to fly', said Erzuth. 'Good', said Lily. 'I'll just spell-paint it the right colour and bind it.' She waved her wand in the air, and 'pop', the boulder looked exactly like the dragon egg which was safely under the table at her cottage. And importantly, you couldn't move it at all!

'Now', she said, 'Magic has tied it to Dragonmount, and I don't think anyone holding it will be able to let go. Is there somewhere Bill and I can hide and still see what's happening?' The dragons showed her a little cave where rocks had gathered, near the top of Dragonmount. 'Wonderful', she said. 'Right, if we're all ready, dear Rezu could you please start mind-talking as loudly as you can like a baby dragon. Everybody else, hush!! Especially you, dear dragon children, we want to keep you safe!'

It was a lovely afternoon. The sun was warm, the grass was green, and the dragons had hidden themselves flat on the hillside. They were invisible! Lily the Witch, Bill and Rags were watching from their cave, and all was quiet. Then Rezu began mind-shouting in a squeaky voice as though she was very small and very afraid. 'Help me, oh help me, I'm lost! Help me!' To begin with, nothing happened. The sky remained blue, the birds sang, and all was peaceful. 'Help me! Oh, help me, I'm lost!' repeated Rezu. And then, although you couldn't really point at anything and say 'That's changing', there *was* a change. Blackness was creeping in at the edges of the sky, the sun was like a furnace, and the birds had stopped singing. 'Yes! It's working', said Lily. 'He's heard you call, Rezu! He'll be here soon'.

And so he was. Everything went still and silent, as a sparkling black figure flew towards them at frightening speed, flashing around its edges just like a thunderstorm, and scattering little sparks as it came. 'Ready, everyone?' said Lily out loud, avoiding mind-speak while Rezu continued to cry 'Help me, oh help me, oh help!'. The blackness dropped from the sky towards the boulder-egg, and grasped it. There was a glittering haze around the egg and then a roar of rage from Ludo.

At once both Erzuth and Rezu reared up on the side of Dragonmount, breathing fire and smoke. With another roar, he strained to lift the boulder into the sky and fly away with it, but he couldn't. Lily the Witch waved her wand, and a spider's web of bright light flashed around Ludo, but with an even bigger blaze of energy he managed to let go of the egg, and as he let go he bounced straight up into the sky, and fire lit the top of Dragonmount as the dragons chased him through the air. 'You can't stop me!' he howled as he rose in the sky. 'I am brother to the sun!' and he met their flames with flames of his own.

Erzuth screamed and fell out of the sky, landing heavily near Lily, who waved her wand over the wounded dragon. 'You'll be fine' she said, and then while Ludo was laughing at Erzuth, Rezu flew round and roasted him from behind. He screamed in his turn, and flew away with Rezu chasing him towards the horizon. 'You elves!' Lily mind-spoke. 'Now!' and they cast an elf-spell which turned the sky magically, totally black. Without the sunlight, Ludo could no longer fly, and he crashed into the stream beside Lily's cottage, and then great clouds of steam hid everything.

Lily the Witch pointed her wand down the mountain so she could see her home. We wouldn't have been able to see her cottage from high on Dragonmount, because nearly everything was dark, but Lily was a witch, and witches can do things like that. The elves had surrounded Ludo, who was covered in pond-weed and spitting out lots of little fish, and screaming 'I'm drowning'. He hated water.

Lily breathed a sigh of relief and smiled. 'My elves have captured him and they will hold him as long as we need', she said. She mind-spoke to the elves, who by now were climbing all over Ludo. 'We shall all be with you very soon, but I must bring Bill and Rags with me', she said, 'so I'm going to ask for some help from my old friends here', and she sent a mind-picture of the dragons. The elves all cheered. Turning to Erzuth, Lily was delighted to see her old friend standing upright again. 'Thankyou', said Erzuth. 'Ludo is much too strong for one old dragon'. 'Almost too much for two dragons!' said Rezu. 'And maybe a little too much for me on my own, too!' said Lily, 'But all together, with my elves, you my old friends ('and with us helping too', said three baby dragons – for yes, the Dragon Child's egg had hatched under Lily's table at the cottage), we have put a stop to his wickedness'.

'We can carry you and your friends down the mountain', said Rezu. 'You can trust us, for we have had to do far harder jobs!' 'We'll come too', chirped the two nearby baby dragons, flying up in wobbly circles. 'And me', said a small voice. Rezu smiled a dragon-smile. The little dragon back at the cottage was ready to fly. The big dragons stood tall. Lily and Bill each climbed onto a scaly back, and Rezu picked up Rags very carefully in her front claws (not without some shivering and very worried looks!) and then they leaped into the air.

What a ride! With the wind whistling through their hair, and with shimmering light from the wand held high by Lily the Witch, they soared on the backs of dragons, down the mountain, over the hills and the woods, and then landed gently on the green at Melody Lane just as the elves relaxed the magic, the sun reappeared and the blackness faded away. Erzuth and Rezu were very cautious about being so close to the water, but they trusted Lily and soon relaxed.

At the stream, elves were still climbing all over Ludo, binding him in bright energy. He was too wet to fight them, and instead grew smaller and smaller, and his flashes of energy grew weaker and weaker, until his efforts faded away and he shivered and sat up, looking very sorry for himself. 'He is drained', said Lily. 'I have bound up his ability to fly, and he will have to walk home. Hopefully that is the end of his wickedness'. She waved her wand as he stood up and turned, and started walking, and then a big magic boot appeared in the air and kicked him hard in the bottom.

Ludo squealed and fell over, and then stood up and turned to glare at Lily, before walking unsteadily away. The elves cheered and stamped their feet, and all the dragons - even the two littlest ones - blew fire and smoke straight up into the air. Rags jumped into Bill's arms, and Bill kissed him firmly on the nose! 'Now' he said. 'How about apple pie for all, and custard for dragons! Catnip for the cats and treats for a certain little dog!' 'Of course, said Lily. 'But before we do anything else there is someone who wishes to say hello', and she went into her cottage, and reappeared with a little dragon coloured gold and red. He flew in a very wobbly way to greet his mother Rezu, and then Erzuth, before joining the other baby dragons, who made a big fuss of him.

And then everyone – Lily the Witch, Bill, dragons, elves, and Rags - sat down on the grass beside the stream and chatted in the evening sunlight. Lily waved her wand to make refreshments, and much later, after long and happy conversations about everything from eggs to Easter, and cats to custard powder, the elves returned to their little hill, and Rags and the cats returned to the kitchen to curl up and nap, leaving everyone to say their farewells.

'Little mother', said Erzuth, 'we must meet more often. I have greatly enjoyed today's adventure, and I am so pleased that my very good friend Rezu has her family together again'. 'It has certainly been an adventure', said Lily, 'and we too enjoyed it, especially working with you to catch that rascal Ludo'. 'Yes', said Bill. 'Let's hope he's learned his lesson. Certainly I have learned more today about dragons, mind-speaking, Dragonmount, and custard, than I ever dreamed possible'. He hiccup'd.

And they all laughed.

Micky Black

LILY THE WITCH AND WILLOW THE WISP

Lily was sitting in her garden. It was a warm summer morning full of sunshine, and her cats Honey and Marmalade were playing catch with a woodpecker. Rags was flying in circles higher and higher over the cottage, when suddenly he landed and said 'Bill's here' just as Bill himself arrived, and Rags stood up to have his head scratched, wagging his tail. Bill looked worried. 'I need to talk to you', he said. 'Something keeps whispering that I must go to the woods'. ' 'Something?' said Lily. 'You mean someone? And what for?' Bill scratched his head and looked around over his shoulder. 'I don't know', he said. 'Why whisper to me? Why am I supposed to go to the woods, and why right now? I just don't know.'

Lily the Witch frowned. 'Well', she said, 'Come in and talk about it. I'd offer you one of my new butterfly cakes, but they've turned into seagulls, and most of them have flown away!' When they got to the kitchen there were still one or two seagulls flying round and round and squawking, and making an awful mess, so Lily waved her hand at them, but instead of flying away they landed on her! 'Bother!' she said. 'Forgot my wand!' and she picked it up and with a quick flick she sent them flying through the door and away. Now, seagulls are not the cleanest of birds, so she had to magic the entire kitchen clean, too!

Then, each with some of Lily's apple pie, and with Rags and the cats at their feet, they sat looking at each other with puzzled expressions. 'So tell me more about these whispers – what did they say? Where were you? Who...' 'Stop, stop', smiled Bill, waving his hands. 'You're making me giddy! Now, let me see. The first time it happened, I'd been out in my garden, and when I came back indoors, I felt as though there was someone watching me. I turned to look, but there was nobody there. And that's when I heard the whispers, sounding like 'Willow, willow'. I looked everywhere but I couldn't find anything. Or anyone! But then I heard it again. Just over my shoulder - 'Willow, willow'. There was still nobody there, but somehow I just knew the voice wanted me to go to the woods – and I don't know why'.

Lily frowned and gazed for a while out of the window. 'Well,', she said after a while. 'Maybe I have some answers. Maybe... I've had to guess some of it, but let's see if it makes sense.' 'Oh dear,' said Bill. 'Is it complicated?' Lily sighed, 'Yes, I suppose it is', she said, stroking Honey's head. 'Well, it all began a long time ago, when there were fairies'. 'Fairies?' said Bill, and a smile lit up his face, 'Really?' 'Well, yes, really there were fairies', said Lily the Witch. 'There were fairies for every plant, every type of growing green thing. One for daffodils, another for roses, one for bluebells - a daffodil fairy, a rose fairy, a bluebell fairy and so on. More fairies than you could ever count. They were lovely little people with wings, caring for the plants whose names they shared. The elves and the fairies were good friends, and helped each other whenever they could. Then one day something horrible happened!'

'Oh dear', said Bill, 'It's usually at this point you start talking about Ludo, so I guess he has a part in this story, too', and he took another piece of pie. 'Yes', she replied 'I'm pretty sure he caused all the sadness. If anything upset the plants, the fairies and the elves worked together to put it right. If the plants were dry, they magic'd rain. Too wet and they made it drier.'

'Ludo would have been annoyed about that. He always wants to be in control, and for someone else to manage the weather would have made him furious. He may only be able to fly when the sun shines, but he is very strong and can be really nasty, and because he couldn't catch the elves, he punished the fairies. Nastily. He made them all disappear!'

'There were fairies everywhere until one very hot day, when all the plants and the trees would have been really uncomfortable, and I think the fairies decided they had to visit my elves, and work magic with them to make things cooler'. 'And you think Ludo found out about it, and got cross?' said Bill. 'Yes', said Lily. 'He likes it hot and always wants his own way, and I think he decided to catch all the fairies as they came to see my elves, using his magic to turn them all into the plants they loved. So he turned the daffodil fairy into a daffodil, the rose fairy into a rose. And so on. And I think he caught every fairy except Willow'.

'But how could Willow have escaped?' said Bill. 'Willow would almost certainly have been the last to arrive, she can be very dreamy. And so he missed her. And ever since then she has wandered around on her own. The last and only fairy. Lovely as ever, but so sad. And I think she's been fading gently and slowly away. A weeping willow. You were so lucky to hear her. Ludo has done some horrible things, but if I'm right, that's one of the worst! And he did it when I went to see the Fairy Queen. I couldn't find her or the King, and sadly, I haven't seen any fairies since.'

'But how can I hear Willow if I can't even see her?' said Bill. 'Because she likes you', said Lily. Bill sat and thought. 'If they've all been trapped, then she may be our only chance to rescue them!

And we must find them and set them free!' 'Yes, of course', said Lily. 'But I'm only guessing what happened, and so I can't be sure what to do about it!' 'Hmm' said Bill. 'Well, if Willow is trying to talk with me, and I can hear her, and I know who she is, maybe we can get her to tell us?' They sat quietly together. 'Willow', said Bill. Nothing happened.

Then, a little later, when Lily the Witch and Bill were just chatting about any and everything, there was a whisper from the doorway. 'Willow, willow, willow'. But you still couldn't see anything. Rags carried on dozing. Honey stretched, and only Marmalade looked up, and stared, before getting to her feet and going quietly to the doorway, then sitting down and purring. 'Aaah', said Lily. 'That's a very good sign - cats love willow, especially the furry buds we call pussy willow. And if Marmalade and Willow like each other too, maybe you're right and that's the way to do it'.

There was a long silence while they sat and thought about it all, then Lily jumped to her feet, and her chair fell over with a crash, causing the cats to jump and Rags to bark. 'Yes, of course it is, Bill.', she said excitedly, 'you're right! We must help Willow to talk! It's been so long since the fairies were here, and we've all missed them. Especially the elves miss them. And you may have found the answer! Thankyou!!' And without saying another word, she ran out, through the garden, and over to the little hill where the elves lived. She knocked hard on the green door, it opened, and she disappeared inside.

Bill sat quietly by himself, thinking. He looked at Marmalade, still purring in the doorway. 'Willow', he said, but there was no answer. 'Willow', he tried again, and this time there was a reply, as gentle as leaves rustling in a breeze. 'Willow. Help. Willow'. Marmalade stood up and waved her tail. Honey stood up and wandered over to be with her friend. Rags stayed dozing at Bill's feet (dogs only really notice willow when they chase sticks). 'Willow', said Bill, 'we are trying hard to help you and all the other fairies. Please don't go away. We need to talk. Be strong'. The reply was definitely stronger. 'Willow. Help'.

Lily was sitting inside the elves' home, talking with them about Willow, and how she was whispering her name, how maybe they could set the fairies free; and how she thought Ludo must have trapped them. It was very dark under the hill, but that was alright because witches and elves can see in the dark. Elves are normally happy little people, but just talking about Ludo made them very cross, and they stamped their feet (elves always stamp their feet when they're cross or excited). If it was Ludo, they wanted him punished, and there was a lot of shouting and arguing. 'No, no, just listen. We must work together' said Lily. 'We must all share this adventure, I can't do it on my own'.

So the elves quietened down, and listened carefully as she told them what she hoped to do, and when she finished they clapped, and danced, and sang, and cheered - they missed the fairies and wanted to help set them free. 'Remember', said Lily the Witch, 'Ludo will be very cross if he finds out, and he will do everything he can to keep the fairies locked away, so you must keep everything secret. Don't even whisper about it unless you're here where he can't see or hear you!' The elves promised, and Lily smiled and thanked them, then she walked back to her cottage. The day was already hot and sunny. 'I hope it doesn't get warmer', she said, 'or we'll need some storms!'

In the kitchen, Marmalade and Honey were sitting in the doorway together and purring loudly, and although you couldn't see anyone else, you just knew someone was with them. Bill was sitting by the fireplace, and still trying to talk with Willow even if he couldn't see her. 'Willow, we are going to help get all the fairies free. I promise', he said. Then Lily came back from the little hill. She looked at where the cats were sitting, and smiled. 'My elves are so happy that we found you, Willow, and they can't wait for us to free your brothers and sisters', she said. But we really do need to talk with you first. So I'm going to find some nectar for you, to make you stronger. And I need the custard powder'. 'Do fairies like custard?' said Bill. 'Not much', Lily replied, 'but we need to can see who we're talking with'.

Lily fetched custard powder, tipped some in her hand, and walked quietly over to where her cats were sitting. Then she blew the custard powder into the air, and it floated down like mist, landing on a little shape. A little girl. Dressed in rags. With wings. Standing, smiling at them. 'Willow', she said. Marmalade stood on her hind legs as if to hug Willow, and to her surprise fell right through her and landed with a bump on the floor. Honey backed away. Willow looked surprised, and then started laughing, and as she laughed she seemed to become more real. Bill and Lily laughed too, and as Marmalade picked herself up, Willow reached down and stroked her, and the little cat arched her back and purred louder than ever.

Lily smiled at Bill. 'You were right', she said. 'Willow and my cats are already friends. Willow', she said, 'you are stronger, but you're still just a wisp. A dream. If it wasn't for my custard powder, we couldn't even see you. What we really need to see is the real you, not custard! And we need very much to talk with you. Now, here is a bowl of nectar. I shall leave it next to you. Do try to take some, it will quickly make you stronger, and once you're strong again to give us some answers, we'll help free your friends'.

She turned to Bill. 'You and I have a job to do. We need to visit the woods, just as Willow wanted you to this morning. Then, it was a mystery. Now, thanks to your idea, I think we know what we need to find, and why. Let's go! Honey and Marmalade, please look after Willow. Keep her very safe, and help her wherever you can. And if Ludo comes here looking for Willow and throwing sunspots, you know what to do', she smiled. 'Eat them!'.

Lily and Bill walked with Rags along Melody Lane, over the old stone bridge, and into the woods. 'Please tell me where we're going?' he said. 'If you wait a little longer', said Lily the Witch, 'I'll show you!', and she led the way deeper and deeper among the trees, which grew bigger and thicker and darker and darker the further they went. And then all at once there was a big round open space, with a mound in the middle, many pretty toadstools standing in a ring, sunbeams shining down through the trees, and beautiful birdsong. Bill and Rags both stopped and stared. 'This is the place I must have been looking for when I came here, even if I didn't know then', he said. 'It's a very special place', said Lily. 'It's the last true Fairy Ring in the whole world. We can talk here and probably Ludo couldn't hear us!'

Everywhere there were flowers, plants, and bushes, and trees of every imaginable shape, size and colour. 'Look around' said Lily. 'I think all the fairies – all except Willow - are here, but locked away. We need to unlock them. And to do that we need Willow's help!'

'So, why did she want me to come here this morning?' said Bill. 'I think Willow wanted you to find this ring, to see if it was safe, and tell me', said Lily. 'We must go back and make her smile'.

And then the sun flared brightly and a hot breeze blew. 'Isn't that Ludo?' said Bill. Rags lay down and shivered.

'He won't know we're here', said Lily. 'Fairy Rings are very special and he won't be sure even if he guesses. Let's just hope Honey, Marmalade and Willow are safe! If he suspects she is nearby, he will use sunspots to try and find her. My cats can eat the sunspots, but I just hope Willow sees the danger she's in!'

They waited a few heartbeats, until the awful feeling had passed. The sky cooled, but the Ring, which had been full of birdsong, stayed silent. Lily looked at Bill. 'Count to ten', she whispered, 'and then let's go back to my cottage as quietly as possible'. They both counted silently, and then, sharing a nod, they left the ring, with Lily the Witch leading the way and Rags walking beside Bill. The trees gradually thinned until they were looking out at the old stone bridge, and beyond it Melody Lane and Lily's cottage.

The hot breeze strengthened again and the sky was like an oven ('he hasn't gone far', said Bill. 'Maybe he really does think there's a fairy somewhere'). The friends crept across the bridge, and tiptoed along Melody Lane, keeping to the shelter of the trees. 'Follow me', whispered Lily the Witch. 'I know a little path that leads to my orchard. That way he's not likely to see us'. They found the opening to the path, between two trees, and walked under many heavy branches, among tall grasses and bushes, and around big rocks. 'Nearly there', whispered Lily, and sure enough, there was the orchard. 'Quiet now', she said, picking up Rags, and they crept from tree to tree until they could reach the kitchen door. But when they did, it was open, and the cottage was empty! Willow, Honey, and Marmalade had vanished!

Bill and Lily stood outside and looked at each other, then tiptoed into the kitchen, and quietly shut the door. 'Now what?' said Bill. 'Let's hope they, are safe', said Lily. 'If Willow felt that Ludo was nearby, they may have hidden somewhere. Let's hope they're safe' – and just at that moment there was a loud sparkling sound from outside. 'Sunspots!' said Lily. 'Rags, it's usually my cats who eat them, but you must help us today!' Soon, black and sparkly fingers were trying to sneak under the kitchen door. Rags didn't wait, he gave a little growl and jumped on them, crunching them with his sharp teeth, one then the other until they'd gone.

Lily waited a moment, then looked out of the window. The sunspots were disappearing down the garden, and the roasting heat was fading. 'He must have decided there aren't any fairies here', she said. 'Let's wait a few minutes then we go and look for them. Fairies love elves, so I hope I know where they are!' A few minutes later, having told Rags 'You'd better stay here, in case there are any more sunspots', Lily the Witch took Bill over the garden to the elves' little hill. 'If she's there, Willow will be wanting to see you', she said.

They knocked 'tap a tap tap' on the elves' green door. It opened a little so the elves could see who knocked, and when they saw Lily and Bill it opened wide, they went in, and it closed behind them. Lily waved her wand to make some light (witches, elves and fairies may see in the dark, but Bill couldn't), and stopped. There, surrounded by smiling elves and smiling herself, and with Marmalade in her arms and Honey by her feet, was Willow. But not the almost-invisible Willow from Lily's kitchen. This was a happy Willow who had taken nectar, and you couldn't see through her at all. The cats purred like distant thunderstorms.

Lily walked over to Willow with a big smile on her face and hugged her, and Bill smiled and waved. 'Welcome back, Willow', they said together. 'We were worried Ludo had found you'. 'He nearly did', Willow replied. 'Without Marmalade and Honey, and my lovely friends the elves I would have been lost, but the Head Elf ran and found us just in time, and brought us here. I am so happy to be back among friends'.

After telling everyone what they'd found, Lily and Bill took Willow back to the cottage. Rags was so pleased to see them that he danced up and down, while Honey and Marmalade looked at him as if to say 'Oh, really, you even have to dance?' Soon, apple pie was on the table, nectar was in Willow's bowl, and the animals were fed.
Once they were all comfortable, Bill smiled at Willow, who was sitting cross-legged on the floor with Marmalade and Honey, and said 'It is so nice to see you looking more like a fairy, and not just a wisp. We worried about you, and we want to hear your story, and now you know what we've seen, we need you to tell us how we can free the rest of the fairies too'. There was a silence for a few moments, and then Willow began: 'I will tell you what I know', she said. 'Once upon a time we fairies were all one big happy family. Yes, there were many of us, but we loved each other and we cared for our plants, just as our King and Queen cared for us. Our plants, all around the world, were happy and healthy. If any of them had problems, we did what we could to help, and if we fairies weren't strong enough, we knew we could ask the elves to use magic to

make things better. Then if they made rain, the plants were happy. And if they needed warmth we could make them happy too. We often met at the Fairy Ring in the wood, or in one of the other Fairy Rings around the world (she stopped and sobbed 'I'm so sad they aren't there anymore!') - to talk about our plants, to sing and dance, talk and eat and be happy, and sometimes the elves came as well'.

'Then one summer, the sun shone hotter and hotter and hotter. The fairies weren't happy, because the plants were uncomfortable. Eventually those with the most soft and sweet plants – violets, bluebells – decided to talk with the elves. So they came towards the little hill. And behind them came all the other fairies - buttercups, roses, hawthorns and all the others, until I was left trailing a long way behind. I never hurry, because Willows are gentle, slow-moving trees. But being last meant I saw it all. As the fairies arrived here, Lily Witch, and before they could knock on the door, that wicked Ludo trapped them, each and every one – they didn't even have time to struggle before he magicked them into their own plants. All my lovely friends! And neither you nor the elves knew they were there...'

Willow sobbed. Marmalade licked her and Honey stood and rubbed her arm with her head. 'He told them all he was going to plant them in the Fairy Ring in the woods, and they'd stay there for ever. Then he gathered them all up, and flew off with them, and I think that's where he went, and where they have turned into plants. I have lost the friends I loved. He said he'd throw the crowns of the King and Queen into the lake in the middle of the Ring so they too were lost. I don't know how he missed seeing me. Willows weep. Maybe I was weeping, and he doesn't like water. Once I heard what he planned to do, I hid and kept still next to one of my trees. I have been so lonely ever since. And now? I am so happy to be with you, and I hope you can bring my friends back.' Lily and Bill looked grim, and gave her a big hug.

'That was a lovely but very sad story', said Lily the Witch. 'You have been very brave. We are so pleased to be with you, and we'll do everything we can to find and free your friends. What happened was wicked. 'But there's one thing that I don't understand', said Bill. 'There is no lake in the Fairy Ring – we were there this morning. There's a mound, not a lake.'

Willow looked into the garden and sobbed. 'It has been a long time', she said. 'Much will have changed. But I just know the fairy crowns are there, among my friends. Somewhere'.

'So how do we get your friends back?' said Lily. 'That's simple', said Willow. 'You hold the crowns and wish three times. But I could never find the crowns. Once you have them you can free all my friends…' Bill looked at Lily. 'I think my wand will give us the answer', she said. 'We must go back to the Ring with Willow, and without Ludo seeing us. Now would be a good time, because we know he's just flown away, and it's getting dark. Let's go!'

'You cats, please take care of the cottage while we are gone'. Marmalade looked at Honey and both of them purred loudly, as the friends set off for the Fairy Ring. It was nearly dark, and the sun was sleeping ('This is the best time to go' said Lily 'because since the sun cooked him Ludo can only fly when the sun shines'). She waved her wand to make enough light and they set off along the secret little path along Melody Lane, with Rags leading the way, and Willow holding Bill's hand. They walked carefully along the lane, over the old stone bridge, and into the woods. 'Be sure to stay close', said Lily. 'Will you have enough light to see what you're doing?' said Willow. 'Trust me' said Lily the Witch.

Eventually, when they arrived at the Ring, it was completely dark, and only Lily's wand threw any light. 'We won't see much if we search now', said Bill. 'Especially for something that's been lost for all that time'. 'Watch', said Lily, and with her wand she drew a circle in the air around them. Suddenly there was a flash and they were all flying upwards. 'Bother!' said Lily. 'Wrong spell!' and when she waved her wand again they were gently back on the ground and they could see as if it was daylight. 'Now', she said, 'walk away from each other'. And when Bill and Willow walked away, the light stretched to cover them all. They could see very well. 'Right', said Lily. 'Let's walk to the middle'. Willow stopped, looked, and said 'it was not like this. there was a beautiful lake, with thrones in the middle on a little island'. She paused. '...and I remember the lake was much the same size as this mound'.

Lily stopped immediately and her eyes opened wide. 'The same size?' she said. 'You'd better stand well back. Now... I wonder…' She waved her wand over the mound. It groaned and shivered, but stayed still. She tried again, and it groaned more loudly. 'Oh come on', she said, and as she waved her little stick higher and higher, very slowly one side of the mound heaved into the air, while the other sank into the ground. 'It's upside down', she said. 'Ludo has been very clever! He hid your lake underneath the mound!'

Willow and Bill stared in surprise, and Rags barked. Soon, the lake was complete, shining in reflected light, and in the middle was a little island, with two shining golden thrones. 'Now', said Lily the

Witch. ‘Willow, we need to know how to find the crowns if they are here’. Willow stretched out her arm, on which was a bracelet. ‘All the fairies wear one of these. They were given to us by the Queen, long before the sadness with Ludo. They are tied to the crowns. If we throw this in the water we shall find them’.

Bill took the bracelet, pulled some string from his pocket, tied the bracelet on one end, then threw it into the lake. The earth trembled. Waves appeared on the lake. And when he pulled on the string, with it came Willow’s bracelet, and tangled up with it was a large bag.

Bill pulled the bag to the shore. Lily picked up the bag, and said ‘Willow, you should be the one to see what is inside’. Willow tiptoed toward the bag, reached inside, and pulled out – two identical golden crowns. She cried and cried. ‘It is the fairy crowns’, she said. ‘My friends, we can reach you. At last!’ It was at that moment that there was a rustling in the bushes on the other side of the Fairy Ring, and sparks began flying into the air.

Lily the Witch turned to Bill and Willow. ‘We all know who that is. He must have walked here. He cannot fly at night. Right’, she said, 'Bill - take this ring, and if I have problems, rub it hard as quickly as you can, it calls my shadows’. Bill looked confused. ‘I’ll explain later’, she said. Turning quickly, she said 'Willow, I'll explain to you later as well. Only you know how to find the fairies. When the time is right, use the crowns to call your friends’.

The evening was getting very warm, and she turned to face the sounds which were growing louder and louder, as more and more sparks flew through the air. Sunspots! Moments later a dark shape jumped into view, a shape very like Lily, but with a sparkly black outline, a very fierce face and shining eyes, and in one hand a blaze of purple energy which threw sparkly shapes into the air as he walked. It was Ludo.

He wore a nasty smile and looked as though he had no cares in all the world. Lily the Witch looked around. Bill and Rags were standing together, but Willow and the bag containing the fairy crowns had disappeared! 'I knew you were here when I saw that flash!' he rumbled in an angry voice. 'Give me the crowns!' She could feel the heat from him although he was still quite a distance away. 'I don't think so', she said, waving her wand in the air, and a curtain of clear, bright energy grew in front of him. 'Ha!' he shouted 'You can't stop me!', as he threw more and more sunspots into the air. They hissed and crackled as they flew, and screamed as they hit Lily's energy curtain. More and more sunspots were thrown, and Lily was sweating, but the energy curtain stayed in place. Then Ludo grew closer to them, and reached out with his free hand to touch the curtain, which shook and shivered.

Lily took some little glass balls from her pocket, and threw them at him, singing and waving her wand in the air. The glass balls went bang as they flew, sending out showers of water, and there were loud hissing noises as Ludo was soaked. He screamed and shook, but then he threw handfuls of energy at the curtain, and it started to crack.

'Now, Bill', Lily panted, and Bill rubbed the ring. Immediately three faces appeared in the air, and grew immediately into girls just like Lily. Then they rushed to help her. The first girl waved a wand just like Lily's and a great wave of water washed through the curtain and hit Ludo, who screamed in pain. The second girl threw a great big mesh of plants and vines which wound round him from head to foot, and as the third girl waved, a strong wind roared across the Fairy Ring and blew him over, leaving Lily the Witch and Bill untouched. Soon, Ludo was as still as a tree. A bright moon shone down on everyone. And - silence.

Willow suddenly reappeared next to Bill, who jumped. 'Who are her friends?' she said. ‘They were amazing!’ 'They’re my shadows', said Lily the Witch. 'They are just me. Witches can be all sorts of things - sometimes they can just be copies of themselves! One of my shadows cares for the waters, another for all living things, and the third cares for the air and everything in it - and I needed all the help I could get if I was to tie Ludo down, he is very strong' (listening to this, Ludo groaned and sparks flew, but he couldn't move). 'But my shadows and I worked together and we were stronger!'

Willow clapped. ‘Everything fitted together so well', she said. 'The bracelet which we used to gather the crowns can also hide me’, she said. ‘So I picked them up and used it’. Lily the Witch and the three shadows smiled. Then Willow held the crowns high in the air. ‘Crowns’, she said, ‘I wish' (the waves on the lake bounced around); 'I wish' (and the plants on the little island shook very hard too); 'I wish my sisters and brothers were with me as before’. There was a flash and a bang, and Ludo groaned and wriggled but he could not speak or break free. All round the Ring there were strange noises and flashes of light, and many of the plants waved as if in a breeze. Then a rainbow grew in the lake and seemed to fill the Ring, as down it walked hundreds – no, thousands – of fairies, led by their King and Queen. Willow gave them the crowns and they put them on, and the Ring filled with sweet music.

Lily the Witch and her shadows curtsied to the fairy King and Queen, and then took time to quietly talk with them, before they all (the Fairy King, the Fairy Queen, Lily the Witch, Bill, Rags and of course Willow) turned to Ludo, who was looking furious but powerless. 'What you have done to these gentle people cannot be forgotten', Lily said. 'And yet they forgive you. You have been really wicked. Now go, and live right!' and she waved her wand, then with a crash of thunder, flashes of lightning, heavy rain, and strong winds, Ludo was blown away into the night. Afterwards, with a soft glow and the sound of chiming bells, Lily's three shadows started spinning and vanished too.

The dancing and celebration at the Fairy Ring lasted for a very long time. Willow, Lily and Bill were heroes, and every single fairy came to say thankyou. The King and Queen gave them all the Freedom of the Kingdom of Fairies, and said they would always be welcome at the Ring. Willow was made a Princess and cried. 'Please give our love to the elves', said the King, and the Queen gave both Bill and Lily golden pendants. 'If you ever need help from the Fairy Kingdom, just wish three times' she said. Lily put her pendant around her neck. It seemed to take away all the pain, tiredness, and aches she'd had from fighting Ludo. 'It's beautiful', she said. Bill was proud. Even Rags had an award – a golden collar, with which he danced around and barked. And there were delicate gold collars to take home for the cats.

They had enjoyed their party at the lake, but eventually, yawning, it was time for Lily the Witch and Bill and Rags to leave. 'My cats will probably miaow for hours', smiled Lily, 'but they will be pleased to see us, I know. What an adventure! All the world's plants will feel much better for having their fairies back again, and I think Willow will spend ages caring for the willow trees which live on my elves' home! In the morning I must go and see the elves, and tell them all about it!'

Then the Fairy Queen, smiling, waved her hands. A rainbow stretched out in front of them, and they were quickly and quietly carried home. The night was nearly over, and the sun was just starting to show his face over the village when they reached her cottage. The elves came out of their home and sat on the grass and clapped as they listened to the story. 'I suppose', said Bill, 'that now the world is healthy once again, Ludo has been punished and the fairies are back, there will be fairies everywhere'. 'Yes', said Lily, smiling and giving him a hug. 'Everything will be happier now. What an adventure!'

Micky Black

LILY THE WITCH AND THE BOOK OF SHADOWS

‘59, 58, 57...’ *woof*

‘56, 55...' *woof*

‘54, 53...’ Lily the Witch was counting all the seconds in a minute, sitting on a sunflower and watching unicorns jump over her garden gate. Rain was falling upwards and the moon was dancing with the sun. Sounds like a daydream? You’re right. Lily was nearly asleep with her head in her hands, sitting in the sunshine at her kitchen table. And what was the noise? That was Rags her little dog. He’d been sitting by her feet for ages, just waiting for his lunch. And he was very tired of waiting!

WOOF! Rags jumped onto Lily’s lap and started licking her nose. That quickly woke her up! 'Ooh - what? Who? Oh, Rags', she said, rubbing the little dog's head. 'You made me jump. I was having a nice dream - whatever is the matter? Was I ignoring you?' Then she looked at the clock on the kitchen wall. 'My goodness', she said, 'is that the time? My best friend Bill will be here, and I haven't even given you lunch!' and she gently put Rags back on the floor. Then she turned, holding his bowl - and came face to face with Bill, who came in just as Rags woke her up. He was smiling broadly. ‘Oh, you did look sweet when he licked your nose!’ he said. Lily frowned then laughed, and finished feeding Rags.

‘So, how are you?’ she said. Bill had a parcel under his arm. ‘I'm fine’, he said ‘and maybe less tired than you’ he said with a smile. 'You bought me a present?' said Lily. 'Well, um, not exactly', he replied. 'It was given to me in Melody Lane, by someone wearing a black coat and hat. They said would I be seeing you? I said yes and they said this was for you.'

Whoever it was, they were in a hurry, because they walked off. So I just brought it in to you. I've been wondering what's in it!' He put it on the table and they both stared at it. Neither of them noticed the quiet mocking laughter or saw the dark figure which walked quietly past the cottage. Lily eventually picked up the parcel and opened it. 'Oh', said Bill, disappointed. 'It's just an old book'. The book really was tired-looking and dusty, and Lily the Witch got up and fetched a damp cloth to wipe the words on its cover before she could read them. 'Poetry?' she said. 'Why has somebody sent me a poetry book?' 'Why, what does it say?' said Bill. And she turned it round so he could read it.

"I hold many dreams, bewitched, and wanting to be free.
But nothing here is what it seems, and witchery is the key".

'Well', he said, 'I wonder what that all means. What dreams?' 'Well, yes, I was daydreaming when you arrived', she said. 'But that can't be anything to do with the book...' and as she spoke, the words on the cover of the book blurred and changed, until it said

"I know you now, I knew you then, when all the world was young.
To free them we must meet again. Your journey has begun!"

'What?', said Bill, and Lily sat down and said nothing for a long moment. 'I don't know. Yet. Let's see what's inside', she said, and she opened the book. 'It's all pictures', said Bill. 'I thought it was a poetry book!' And yes, the book was full of beautiful pictures of animals. But the pictures were very grey, and slowly moving, and the animals all looked at you with sad faces. There were cats and bears, and dogs and dragons. There was even a unicorn, and when she saw that Lily the Witch jumped. 'Emerald! You too!?' she said, and closed the book.

'Oh my, that is a very sad book', she said. 'I wonder who delivered it, and why? Something about this reeks of Ludo, and isn't nice.' She sat and stared at the book with an 'I'm thinking' look on her face. Honey and Marmalade jumped up next to her and rubbed their heads on her shoulders as if to say 'Don't worry, little mother, we'll look after you!'. After a while, she said 'I must go on a journey'. 'Because you saw something in the book?' said Bill, reaching out and touching it. 'Yes', she said. 'Emerald. The unicorn. They are very special, and Emerald was my best friend a long time ago. There was a terrible storm one night, lightning burned her home, and she disappeared. And I haven't seen or heard from her since. Until now'.

'The unicorn?' said Bill, 'But how do you know that is her? How have you heard from her? It's just a book.' 'Mmm, this isn't just any book', said Lily. 'It's the Book of Shadows, and it's dangerous, because inside it there is a different world. But unicorns are magic, so once the Book was opened, she could talk to me even from that picture. She wants me to free everyone in the book, then send it home. But I'd still love to know who delivered it!'

Bill frowned. 'That's difficult' he said. 'It was all quick and unexpected! I was nearly at your gate, and suddenly there was this person in front of me, pushing the parcel into my hands, and turning to go, so I didn't see a face...' Lily frowned. 'Then you came straight in?' 'Yes', said Bill.' He stared at Lily. 'Are you thinking...' and they both jumped to their feet. 'Ludo!' 'Yes but where did he get it from, and why is it here?' said Lily. 'I need to talk with the Head Elf!'

They both walked quickly over to the elves' hill, under the willow trees near Lily's garden, and the Head Elf agreed with them. 'Ludo...' The elves stamped their feet (that's what they do if they get cross) and Bill and Lily went back to the cottage to work out how to save Emerald and all the other animals the Book of Shadows held captive. But Lily had forgotten to shut the Book before they went to see the elves, and when they returned to the cottage, Honey and Marmalade had disappeared. They were staring at them out of the open Book. She sobbed. 'My poor cats - I should have shut the book!'

They sat silently together for a long time, then Bill stood up. 'I am easily pleased, but now I am very angry! I'm going to walk in your orchard!' Lily stood. 'I will come with you!' she said. She closed the Book, and as they walked she put a hand on Bill's shoulder. 'My friend', she said, 'Getting angry makes you strong, but it stops you thinking. And this is a time to think! My cats will enjoy the sun on the windowsill again. And I'm determined to set all the other poor animals free as well! Now, let's go back indoors, and I'll get started on a rescue. Whatever happens, trust me and be patient!'

They returned to the kitchen, both looking fierce but calm, and sat again at the table. The cover of the Book remained the same, but somehow it looked tidier. Cleaner. 'Remember what I said', she said to Bill. Be patient! Then she took out her wand, opened the Book and tapped it, and many sad animal cries filled the kitchen, with a sad 'Little Mother?' at the end, at which she cried 'I'm coming, Emerald!' and launched herself into the Book of Shadows.

Being inside the Book was a very strange, grey feeling. Lily was surrounded by animals of every shape and size. All were grey - there were no colours anywhere. Quickly she was joined by Honey and

Marmalade, then 'Little Mother, is that really you?' rang out and she was nudged by Emerald the unicorn. She hugged her old friend tightly. Then 'Everyone, listen', she said (and because she is a witch, all the animals stopped pushing each other and sat down to listen). 'We are all inside something very dangerous, called the Book of Shadows. Why is it dangerous? Because it doesn't belong in our world, and I need to send it home, but that will be difficult, even for me. I know you all want to be free to live your lives. Living here must be so boring! So I am making you a promise. I will return to my life, because, I have so many things to do. And then I will set you free'. The noise the animals made was very very loud!

Then there was a spell-sound, and the Book was opened by a frightened-looking Bill. That was a bit like seeing someone open the sky! Lily smiled at him. 'I will be back soon', she said. 'Then we must work to free everyone. Now please shut the Book and hide it'. Bill looked relieved, and closed the Book – but then Lily didn't see Ludo sneaking into her kitchen, casting a spell over Bill to hold him still, and pushing Rags into a cupboard. Then Ludo picked up the Book with a wicked smile on his face, and flew away!

Inside the Book, Lily held up her wand and made a spell. But nothing happened. She tried again. Still nothing. And then she knew Bill had magical problems. 'Bother', she said, waving her wand, but instead of making another spell to leave the Book she called her shadows...

Lily is a witch. You know that. But in case you've forgotten about her shadows, there are three of them, and they are like copies of Lily - they look the same, they are all witches, and they always help each other if one of them is in danger. The spell which called them was very strong, and the shadows came quickly to Lily's side. She told them about finding the Book, and they told her what had happened to Bill - they were all very cross. 'Ludo thinks I'm stuck here', she said, 'but he's wrong! It is easier to get into this Book than to get out, and only one of us can go back this time, but once I'm back I will call you too. Then Ludo's in trouble!'

Together they made a circle, and they all twizzled (that's a bit like skipping with a magic rope). There was a loud spell noise, and Lily vanished, then quickly reappeared again in her kitchen, standing next to Bill. 'I thought you'd been caught like your unicorn, and I'd never see you again', he sobbed. 'I'm sorry, I don't know where the Book is. Someone hit me then stole it' he said. 'I know', said Lily the Witch, hearing Rags bark and setting him free.

Rags was so pleased to see Lily again, he barked and danced around her, and was given a long hug, before she said 'Bill, my friend, I must go and talk again with the elves. Please stay here with Rags, and keep the door shut. You know Ludo throws sparkly sunspots to find things If he comes back, Rags can eat any sunspots he throws.

She jumped to her feet without saying another word, and ran from the kitchen, across the garden to where her elves lived. There was a big tree branch leaning against the green door! Lily had to fight to move it out of the way, then, ignoring the big 'DANGER' sign on the door, she knocked hard. The elves opened it a little, then seeing Lily they let her in.

The Head Elf ran up. 'I'm sure Ludo's been here', he said. 'I was about to come and tell you, but the door was stuck somehow.' 'I know', said Lily the Witch. 'Someone had pushed a big branch against it. I think that was Ludo, and I'm pretty sure he gave my friend Bill a parcel this morning. The Book of Shadows!'. The elves hissed. 'He stole my cats, and trapped them in the Book, then he tried to trap me too, then once I'd gone he hit Bill and stole the Book again. I have been inside the Book, and he thinks I'm still there - but he forgot my shadows, and how strong we are. I came back!' The elves turned and nodded to each other.

'Now, I will need your help', she said. There are several things we must do, and quickly. First, I must bring home my shadows, and Honey and Marmalade, and we must free all the animals trapped within the Book. And last (but definitely not least!) I want Ludo found and punished, and the Book of Shadows sent home. It doesn't belong in our world!'

Then she waved her wand, and a big moving picture appeared on one wall of the elves' home. In it, you could see the Book, the animals (and Lily) trapped inside, Ludo stealing the Book again, and Lily's return. The elves looked very fierce, and stamped their feet (elves always do that when they're excited or cross), and Lily said she would bring home her shadows, then every last one of the animals, and she'd need to talk again with the elves and fairies to work out where Ludo and the Book of Shadows were.

And then she went back to her kitchen. When she got there she stood on a stool, waved her hand and made the spell to call her shadows. Nothing happened. Bill tapped her on the shoulder with her wand. 'Shouldn't you have used this?' he said, and before she could speak he waved it. Big mistake. Hot winds blew in through the door, the table caught fire, and snow blew in through the door! 'No - quickly, it only works properly for me', said Lily the Witch. But as she said it, Bill disappeared, and Rags and her wand flew through the air and out of the door, to be snatched by a black figure which then vanished. Ludo!

Without her wand, she could not make any good spells, and without Rags she had nobody to talk with. And once again a horrible mocking laugh echoed quietly down the garden. Lily screamed ‘Nooo’, and almost fell off the stool, sad and cross at the same time. What else could possibly go wrong?

She sat at the kitchen table. No wand, no shadows, no Rags, no Bill, no Honey, and no Marmalade. 'My whole life is upside down', she said, and a little tear ran down her cheek. 'Whatever can I do?!' And just at that moment a deep rumbly voice mind-spoke her. 'Whatever is the problem, little mother? It's not like you to get upset!' It was her old friend Erzuth the dragon, who lived high on Dragonmount. 'Erzuth, my friend' she said. 'I am in horrible mess' - and she described everything that had happened since she went daydreaming that morning, forgot Rags' lunch, and tried to work out where the Book had come from. 'It's only been a little while, and my world is totally upside down'.

'My goodness', said Erzuth. I can see why you are upset! But my friend Rezu and I, and Rezu's young ones, can help you! We know where Ludo has gone - he is very near Dragonmount in some caves! Maybe he’s forgotten that we found him there before!'

Now, both Ludo and Lily can fly. But it was something Lily had forgotten, and so she hadn't flown for ages. Now she suddenly realised how useful that could be! 'If I go to Dragonmount without Ludo knowing!' she said. 'I wonder...' She stood up and willed herself to fly. Then stamped her feet. But her feet weren’t near the floor - she had lifted herself a little way into the air and then dropped back onto the kitchen floor with a crash! She tried again. I can do this, she said to herself, then bang! 'Ouchy!' she said. Her head had hit the kitchen ceiling!

Erzuth rumbled again. 'Little mother', she said, 'are you alright? You were quiet then I heard a bang and you said something?' 'Silly me', Lily said, 'I had forgotten I can fly. That bang was my head hitting the ceiling! If you know where Ludo is, maybe you have saved me. I will come to you right now!' and she walked out of the kitchen door, and wished herself flying. And she was! She flew wibbly wobbly along Melody Lane until she remembered how to do it all properly. Then she flew silently to the purply grey mountain. And met two enormous green dragons. AND three little dragons (two of them green and one reddy-gold). 'I did it!' she said, the dragons breathed smoke, and she landed 'bump' and rolled over and over.

The dragons settled quietly back onto the mountain ('we'd better stay quiet until we know what to do', said Lily the Witch). 'You have plans, little mother?' asked Rezu. 'Well', said Lily, 'I don't have much choice. No wand. Without it my spells are weak. And although I know you, dear Rezu and Erzuth, understand magic and always help, I can't just rely on magic.'

'So I'll do what Ludo does.' The dragons looked at each other. 'What's that, little mother?' they said. 'Cheat', said Lily. 'Ah, dragons don't smile', they said, 'but inside we are laughing!'

'Ludo almost certainly took the Book and what's in it, to his cave-home', said Lily. 'If he's here (and the dragons nodded) he hasn't had time to do anything else. He'll be so proud of himself that he's probably careless', she said. 'I expect he'll have found a way to keep Rags quiet, and I'm hoping he will be laughing himself silly over having the Book and what he's done with it. So hopefully he will be ignoring my wand - he can't really use that anyway, it's tuned to me.' 'Yes, but how will you get your wand back?' said Rezu.

'Well, by acting like a victim', said Lily the Witch, with a wink. In my mind, I can feel Rags and my wand, and they are near. And hopefully Ludo has forgotten Rags can mind-speak, so I shall ask him to help!' She mind-spoke quietly one-to-one with Rags. The first thing she said was 'whatever you do, don't wag your tail!' then she explained what she wanted the little dog to do. 'I'm going to visit Ludo in a little while', she said. 'As soon as you can, get my wand between your teeth and pretend to eat it. Then when I nod, give it to me immediately, and keep out of the way - there may be fireworks!' The dragons were listening carefully. 'We have a suggestion too little mother - one of us can weave a magic calming web over the caves while the other waits, ready to scorch Ludo if he comes out. Don't worry, little mother, we won't toast your toes!' and Lily laughed. 'I'd better get started' she said. 'Things to put right!'.

'We'll show you the caves', said Erzuth, and she and Lily flew through the air, leaving Rezu with the baby dragons until it was safe enough for them to join the party. Erzuth landed out of sight of the caves, in a little valley, and Lily landed with a bump behind her. 'Sorry', she said 'I need to practice. Is that the cave entrance just over that hill?' and Erzuth nodded. Lily quietly mind-spoke one-to-one with Rags. 'We are outside, Erzuth and I. Be ready!', then she started walking, while Erzuth started weaving a magic calming web over the caves. Deep in the caves, Ludo was sitting at a table, with a great big twisted smile on his face. 'At last I have you trapped, Witch', he said looking up at the ceiling and thumping the table. 'Now nothing and nobody can stop me from DOING WHATEVER I WANT!' and he laughed and laughed. Against the furthest wall of the cave, and tied to a wooden post, Rags the little dog lay still, with one eye open and watching Ludo carefully. And on the table in front of Ludo, opened with pictures of Bill, Honey, Marmalade, and the shadows (looking just like Lily the Witch - you would have said it was her!) looking back at him, Ludo was so, so happy. 'At last, at last!' he said, time and time again.

Lily's wand had fallen on the floor as Ludo arrived at the caves, carrying Rags and the Book of Shadows. Rags had picked it up and was holding it in his mouth, pretending he thought it was just a stick, and was playing with it. Ludo looked at him and laughed. 'Lily the Witch won't be using that again!' he said. After a long time, while he laughed, looking in the Book of Shadows, he felt calmer, and shut the Book, the calmness spread, and he stretched his arms above his head, then went to his bed and lay down (still with that silly twisted smile on his face). He was looking forward to flying out into the world the very next day and doing whatever he wanted.

The dragons' calming spell took hold - his eyelids closed then opened again, and felt increasingly heavy, and eventually he just went to sleep and dreamed of flying high over the world, making magical mischief. And snored loudly! It was the snoring that told Lily where to find him, as she went from cave to cave, finding piles of gold coins, jewellery, and treasure everywhere she looked. As she entered the cave where Ludo lay asleep, Rags silently wagged his tail, and stood up with the wand in his mouth. Lily the Witch tiptoed over to where Rags stood, took the wand with a smile on her face, and waved it over Ludo, binding him in sleep. Then she picked up the Book, making sure it stayed closed.

'Your calming spell worked', she mind-spoke to the waiting dragons. 'Ludo is fast asleep and dreaming, and I have my wand and the Book!' She walked over to where Rags was still bound to the wooden post, and freed him. He danced and whimpered with relief. 'I am so pleased to see you again. Thankyou' he mind-spoke, blinking,

'I thought the Book had eaten you alive!' Lily smiled, and said 'The Book on its own can't hurt anyone, let alone eat people. It's the people who use it that cause trouble. The Book is just a doorway to another place, where it was made. Ludo must have stolen it a long time ago. Now, I can send it home once we have freed everything in it. All those poor animals, Bill, my shadows, and of course Honey and Marmalade!' Deep in the Book, there were many smiles.

'So all is well?' said a rumbling voice. Erzuth the dragon was still on patrol outside the cave to make sure Lily the Witch was safe. 'Yes', she said. 'Ludo is asleep, and I have bound him there. I could not have done any of this without your idea and your help!' 'Little mother', rumbled the dragon, 'that is why we are friends - because we like each other and because we are always there for each other. Now, what are you going to do about Ludo?' 'I don't think he can do any more harm while he is asleep', said Lily. 'What I most want to do is to put things back to where they should be - to free everyone and everything held in the Book, all of them trapped where they don't belong. Then I want to send the Book home'.

'Perhaps', said Rezu, who had flown down to join Erzuth once the danger had passed, and the baby dragons were safe, 'Perhaps you should make a spell to bind Ludo in the Book for a while, and let him see what it's like inside? That would be a lesson he could never forget!' 'It would be cruel', said Lily, 'and I won't do cruel!'. Outside the cave, the two big dragons looked at each other. 'You're right', they said together. 'He should not be tamed that way', and they blew smoke into the air as Lily and Rags, the Book - and Lily's wand - emerged from the caves. 'But the Book must go home'.

Lily the Witch put the Book of Shadows on the ground, and drew a circle around it on the grass, with her wand. She stood silent, and thinking, for a while, then she raised her wand and sang a sad, strange little song while twizzling it in the air. There was a sweet, warm wind down the mountain, which ruffled all the pages in the Book, and from the Book came a huge chorus of animal sounds - the roar of lions, the cry of eagles, the bleating of sheep and the trumpeting of elephants, then an endless stream of shadows flew out of the book and vanished like smoke into the air, in every direction.

'They have all gone home', said Lily, smiling. And finally, as the pages of the Book settled and stayed still, several further shadows lifted into the air and stayed there, gradually becoming more real and settling onto the ground – Bill, her shadows, Honey and Marmalade, and Emerald the unicorn. The cats jumped up for a hug with Lily, and then Bill, the shadows and Emerald turned to the dragons and said 'thankyou' before walking over to Lily and hugging her. 'We shall talk long after all this is done' she said. 'But now for the Book'.

The Book of Shadows lay closed and peaceful on the grass. Still on its cover was the mysterious little poem that appeared when this adventure began:

'I know you now, I knew you then, when all the world was young.
To free them we must meet again. Your journey has begun!'

'Well', said Bill, 'much of that poem has come true - the Book must have known you a very long time, if even you had to think hard to remember it! You did have a journey, into the Book and back again, and since you met it again, you have freed all the animals and people within it.' And as he spoke, the poem blurred and changed again, to read:

'Now I must leave and fly with pace, for I have done my part.
No longer tied within this place, once more I have a heart.
Thankyou friends, smiles light your face, my journey home must start'

And the Book of Shadows faded and vanished.

There was a roar from within the caves, then silence. 'He cannot fully wake until we allow it', said Lily. 'But he can feel his loss'. And everyone smiled. 'That', said Emerald, 'is no more than he deserves. I was chained within that book for an eternity, as were many of those chained with me. I have no sympathy for his loss'. Bill and the dragons nodded, and Honey and Marmalade went to Emerald's side and wound their tails around her legs as if to say 'we know, we were in the Book for a little time, but it was so grey and alone.'

They sat together on the warm mountainside, and talked about everything from custard to cats, and dragons to gold. 'We shall guard the treasure Ludo has piled into those caves', said Rezu. 'It is what dragons do best! And whenever you have time to visit, little mother, we can send it back bit by bit to wherever Ludo stole it from.' 'I recognised some of my old jewellery', said Emerald. 'But I have no wish to have it back. Unicorns and jewels really don't need each other!' The cats Honey and Marmalade were so pleased to be free they simply flew around and around for a few minutes (remember they can fly - they are magical cats), while Rags was content just to sit at Lily's feet, and Bill just smiled.

She mind-spoke her elves, back at the cottage, and they were so pleased they cheered and stamped their feet when they heard that everything had returned to normal. Except for Ludo. 'We really can't leave him to sleep for a thousand years', said Erzuth. 'That would be cruel'. 'No', said Lily, 'I have a better idea. Remember, Ludo can only fly in sunlight. So if I weave a spell that puts clouds around him wherever he goes, he will have to walk. And for him, it's a long way home from Dragonmount. It will take him ages - but maybe he will think about what he's been doing and realise how nasty it was'. 'And we will fly around him all the way' said Rezu. 'Just to remind him to behave, and make sure he doesn't find new ways of making mischief! Especially if we have his wand, too...' Lily and Emerald looked at each other. 'That', they said, 'is an excellent idea'.

And so it was. Lily (with the dragons' help!) put a spell on Ludo so that clouds followed him everywhere, then gave his wand to Erzuth and woke him. He was furious at first, but when he realised he had no wand and so could do no mischief, he sulked and started walking. Erzuth followed him, high in the sky, but now and again she swooped through the clouds and scorched his bottom, all the way down from Dragonmount. The shadows hugged Lily the Witch then twizzled and faded into the air. And Lily, Emerald and Bill sat and talked the whole day long, with Honey, Marmalade and Rags sleeping nearby, before promising to meet again soon and share some of Lily's famous apple pie. Then, as the stars came out, Emerald used her very own magic to carry Lily and her friends home.

LILY THE WITCH AND THE BROKEN RAINBOW

Lily the Witch was sitting in her front garden. It was a warm sunny morning, and she was throwing sticks for Rags her little dog. Using magic of course. The sticks were flying high or low, up or down, and spinning like wheels or diving into the stream at the end of her garden, and Rags was having the time of his life and barking. Then one stick landed in the stream just as there was a rainbow flash into the water. 'What was that?' said Lily to herself. 'That was a kingfisher' said a voice, and Rags barked. ‘You didn't say 'hello', said the voice, and she looked around and saw her friend, Bill, walking merrily towards her along Melody Lane.

Lily smiled as he walked up the path to sit with her. 'I love kingfishers', he said. 'There are always lots around your little stream.' 'I expect that's because there are lots of little fish', she said. 'Let's watch for a bit - there's nothing much I need to do today, everything’s quiet, and my elves are probably still snoring. So here I stay, unless there's trouble'. They watched the kingfishers’ rainbow display, and after a while Bill stretched and yawned. 'I love it here', he said, ‘it’s like a jigsaw puzzle, in which everything fits together. Everything. Trees, flowers, bees, fish, kingfishers. And I know they're all lovely and important, but somehow they're the little things, and I always wonder how all the big things fit together, too. You know, the sky, the sea, the mountains. I can't see any of them from my caravan, or even from here’.

'You're right', said Lily. She sat and thought. 'Well, if you like, we can go up the hill at the end of my orchard – you’ll see everything from up there. The sky, the mountains, and the sea. Let's explore. Maybe we'll even see dragons, or rainbows!' She went and knocked on her elves' door to tell them where she was going with Bill (they weren't too happy to be woken up, I can tell you!), gave her cats Honey and Marmalade a hug - 'take care of my cottage!' she said - and then Lily, Bill and Rags walked down the orchard, through a rickety wooden gate, along a stony path, and up the hill. You couldn't really see it from Melody Lane, it was behind the trees, but when you reached the top, you really could see forever.

Bill stopped and stared, puffing a bit from the climb. 'Wow', he said. 'There's your cottage, and the willow trees around the elves' home, and there's Melody Lane and its little stream – yes, and over there are the woods, and in the distance I can see the hills, and there are the mountains. It's like a painting!' 'Aah, the mountains', said Lily. 'I wonder how my dragon friend Erzuth and her family are today?' Lily said - and quick as a flash that familiar voice rumbled in her mind 'Good morning little mother. We are fine. It is a lovely day and we shall be flying around the mountains later. Be happy'.

'There are so many parts of the big jigsaw puzzle!' said Bill. 'At last I can see how some of the big things fit together! What's that blue over there?' 'That's part of the sea', said Lily, 'and that really does go all around the world'. Bill scratched his head. 'I didn't even know that was there', he said. 'It's beautiful.' 'Yes', she said. 'And we must keep it that way.' They sat down on some rocks, and watched the world - the blue sea, the blue sky, the green woods and hills, and the purply mountains. Everything was peaceful, until black clouds started growing around the mountains. 'That looks like rain', Bill said. 'Do rain clouds usually gather that quickly?' Lily frowned. 'Strange', she said. 'The dragons won't want to fly in that! But it won't be coming here - the wind's blowing in the wrong direction, and look, the bees are still flying, and bees are like dragons, they don't fly in the rain'. They watched the darkening sky over the mountains while Rags and the pony lazed in the sun.

'Ah, look', said Bill 'There's a beautiful rainbow, too!' Sure enough a brilliant band of colours was stretching right across the sky, bright against the black clouds. It went high over Dragonmount and out over the sea. 'It's wonderful how the rain does that', he said. Around the rainbow, the gathering black clouds now looked huge and were still growing, and around them lightning flashed like a hundred falling streetlamps. Then bang! All of a sudden, there was an enormous crash (you could hear it even from Lily's hill!), the mountains trembled, half the sky was lit by a big bright flash, and everywhere there were deep rumbling noises. Bill jumped up and pointed, with shock on his face: 'Look - the rainbow's broken in two!' and sure enough, instead of a beautiful curve of colours across the sky, there were two pieces of rainbow where there had been one: One end still soared into the sky like a magic staircase, but it ended like a broken tooth, and the other end was breaking into a million shining pieces, all falling through the air, their colours crashing into the mountain and the sea.

And almost invisible against the black clouds, a dark sparkling figure was flying sneakily away from the mountain.

While a million colours were pouring into the sky from the broken rainbow, the great masses of dark cloud around the mountains grew bigger and bigger as the rocky ground smoked and flickered below. Fiery streaks of lightning flashed and thunder roared. 'What has happened?' mind-shouted an angry Erzuth to Lily the Witch. 'The sky is black and yet it's on fire and laughs, the clouds are crying rain like a roaring river, bleeding every colour at once – and the colours burn everything they touch, even my scales, and they're making our babies cry!'

'The sky laughs!?' said Lily, with a very angry look on her face. 'Rainbows are beautiful, because they soak up all the poisons in the world. But they don't laugh. Now someone (and I can guess who) has cast a spell to break this one, and all the poison it had caught is spilling out everywhere! I must stop it! If it just keeps falling through the sky, the bees, the birds, the flowers, the animals, trees and rivers will die, and people will starve and die too!' She paused. 'No. I must not let that happen!' She stopped to think. Then 'Right', she said, 'go quickly back to your dragon caves, my friends. Rainbows are there to clean everything. If the poisons, the nastiness and the mischief they've collected spreads, your children will be poisoned!'

'But who would do such a terrible thing?' said Bill. 'I think you know', she said. 'The sky doesn't laugh all by itself! I'm sure that was Ludo. He gets his kicks from being more and more dangerous. Now he's making everything sick, and unless I do something that sickness will quickly spread, so please get Rags and your pony back to my cottage as fast as you can. Tell the elves what you've seen. Tell the fairies. Tell everyone! Tell them 'stay indoors!' and I will be back as quickly as I can.'

Lily the Witch waved her wand, there was a shimmering in the air, and with a shimmer she vanished, leaving Bill standing open-mouthed and Rags looking everywhere and whining. Bill looked again towards the mountains, where the blackness and the frightening colours were getting quickly worse, then ran with Rags as fast as he could down the hill and back to the cottage. In the distance, the flashes and rumbles grew steadily louder, and of Lily the Witch there was no sign.

Don't forget, witches are made of magic, which means they do strange things. One of Lily's strange things is that she can make living copies of herself! So one moment you can be talking with her, and the next there's a knock at the door and one, no two, no three Lilys are standing outside waiting patiently to come and say hello to you. She calls these copy people her shadows.

Just like her the shadows are very powerful, and when all the shadows work together they can do many different things all at the same time, and make very strong spells, which is just as well, because Ludo is super-strong too. Sometimes Lily the Witch needs the shadows just to make him behave!

She met her shadows invisibly in the sky above the hill, talking angrily among themselves, then decided that one would go to Dragonmount to calm the sky and start tidying the horrible mess below, one would calm the river which ran down the mountainside, and the sea where they met, one would go and talk with the fairies, and one would hunt for Ludo. Immediately, Lily vanished again, to reappear at the entrance to Erzuth's cave on Dragonmount, high above the hills. She walked inside and Rezu was there too. 'Goodness', said the dragons, 'That was quick!' I wanted to keep you all safe' said Lily, as the three young dragons crooned with pleasure at seeing her. 'But I must know exactly what you've seen'.

'Well, little mother', said Rezu, 'we were all looking forward to flying over the hills today, when a big black cloud suddenly appeared right in front of us. We're used to clouds, but this one made the sky darken so quickly! 'Ah, that's rain', I said, and so we got ready to come home. Then I heard loud laughter in the sky. It wasn't nice laughter, either! I looked around but there was no-one to see, so I wondered if Erzuth was playing games, but when I mind-spoke to her she was in her cave and only just waking up! We decided to stay out a little longer, because it was still warm, but then when the rain came, we started flying home. The rain got heavier and heavier, and then there was a beautiful rainbow! My children love rainbows, because they have the same colours in their eyes. This one was big and bright and so pretty - but that's when the world went bang!'

'There were terrible flashes and noises, as well as the thunder and lightning, and that horrid laughter, and then the strangest thing - the rainbow just broke in two pieces, and pieces of one half started flying through the sky. I have never seen anything like it - the sky looked so wrong just wearing half a rainbow! Then the rain began shining like pieces of rainbow too, and they really hurt when they landed on me. My children were crying. Erzuth must have heard me roar, because she looked out of her cave too, and quickly went back inside. That rain was so painful! And then, just after the rainbow broke, I heard that horrible laugh again, it seemed to come from everywhere! And soon after we were home. But it still stings!'

At that moment there was an enormous crash from outside, and the biggest dragon head you've ever seen appeared in the cave mouth. 'Rezu, it is me, Aznath! Can I come in? Who is that human? Quickly, I'm stinging all over!' Rezu introduced Lily to Aznath, and the dragon children ran quickly to welcome him. 'Little mother', she said, 'this is my children's father. Aznath, this is our little mother, Lily the Witch'. 'Goodness, is that something humans do – have lots of names?' rumbled Aznath. 'Well', said Lily, 'I am who I am, and I hope you and I will be good friends. Now, let me deal with all that stinging', and she waved her wand over all the dragons. 'Aah, that's better', said Rezu and Aznath, as the stinging stopped. 'Me too', mind-spoke Erzuth from her cave. 'And us', sang the three baby dragons.

'Now', said Lily, 'the laughter you heard - was it real, or did you imagine it?' 'I heard it too', said Aznath. 'It was nasty!' Lily stared at the floor. She was cross. 'I think we can all guess who broke the rainbow', she said. 'I will deal with that later, but right now my shadows and I have much to do. You dragons will be safest staying in your caves – there seems to be plenty of room! Now I must go and clean the air.' Aznath and Rezu lay down, and the little dragons huddled between them. 'Take care, little mother' said Rezu, and Erzuth sent a picture of dragons sitting up and looking fierce. 'We will fly to you if you need us', she said.

Lily left the dragon cave and waved her wand to make the rain miss her. It was very pretty rain, but she knew it was poison. She looked up at the broken rainbow, said a few strange words, and again waved her wand. There was a flash, and the broken end of the rainbow glowed first red, then orange, then white, then blue, and there were clouds of bright steam. And when the steam cleared, the end of the rainbow wasn't sharp and jagged, but flat and smooth, and the beautiful but poisonous streams pouring from it into the rain, had stopped.

Lily looked around. The mountainside was a mess! Rainbow colours were everywhere – there were puddles of it, the rocks were covered in it, and the grass was every colour you could think of. Big pieces of rainbow sat like clowns on the mountainside, shimmering in the sunlight, and sadly, wherever you looked there were the bodies of birds and insects, the trees were leaning over, and all the flowers and leaves were flat on the ground.

She mind-spoke the Fairy Queen and told her everything. 'I am so sorry your majesty', she said. 'I hope your fairies were safe. I am cleaning the air. We need to clean up the mountains, and the hills, and return some strength and life to everything - the birds and insects and the plants are desperate. But my shadows and I are strong but need all the help the fairies can give me, and all your loving care, and I know you will want to be here yourself. Soon I must go to find my shadows, who are already mending the waters and making the sky safe - they too will find misery, and work hard to mend it. You elves, I know you are listening, and you know what has happened - now, please help everyone, and if you find Ludo - tell me!'

She turned in a circle, waved her wand and sang in a high pitched voice, and as she turned, the rainbow colours flared then died, leaving everything a shade of grey. Everywhere was the colour of ashes. It was very sad ('just for a while, little mother', mind-spoke Erzuth. 'We will see green grass again'). Lily smiled fiercely. 'I hope you are right, my friend', she replied.

Suddenly, another little rainbow grew beside her, and from it stepped a beautiful and delicate little lady wearing a golden crown. The Fairy Queen. 'My goodness, what a mess', she said. 'Oh dear, oh dear. And to break a rainbow too', she said, looking up. 'We fairies will do everything we can', and she flew into the air to see what had happened. 'So much is broken, and even now, there is so much to mend'. She looked down, but Lily had vanished again.

Lily the Witch re-appeared on a high white cliff beside the sea, next to a deep cave, and as she entered the cave, a group of elves came to greet her. She smiled and hugged them, and they clapped and stamped their feet. 'Today is a sad day', she said. 'You know what has been happening, and who did it. I have started cleaning the air. Our friends the fairies will soon be mending the damage that Ludo has made on the mountains and the hills.

Now it is our turn to help. We are here to clean all the waters. The river which runs down the mountains is very poisoned. We must clean the river, its streams, and sea. And we must start here and now! There is much to do, and many lives will already be in trouble. It is up to us to put things right!' and Lily stepped straight off the cliff, flying quickly down to the sea below - and disappearing into it. The elves looked at each other and then one by one they followed her, jumping from the cliff and falling gently into the water and the worlds beyond.

It was strange in the sea. Lily had made a spell which enabled them all to breathe in the seawater as though they were in some beautiful but strange grassy meadow ('it's cleaner here than it is around the river', said Lily). Her elves joined hands, then they all flew through the water as though they were larks and the sea just a summer breeze.

Inquisitive eyes watched them as they flew by - seals blinked, fish flicked away and then turned to watch, while on the sea-floor crabs and shellfish moved gently about, and huge strands of seaweed beautifully waved in the water. All as if nothing had happened. Lily and the elves knew better, and they swam like a shoal of fish. Then, as they drew closer and closer to the river, the water changed. It became like strange silk, with shining strands and flashes everywhere. Fishes, seals, even a shy octopus were poisoned, floating aimlessly around, and seemed to have no idea where they were or what they were doing.

At the mouth of the river, the water became muddy and like soup. All living things lay lifeless on the bottom. Even the big seaweeds were laying flat. What seemed like a dirty coloured curtain was settling through the water, making everything look foul and still.

Lily sighed, then raised her wand and waved it in a circle up and down, round and round. At first, nothing happened, but then the curtain slowly began to clear. The elves gently floated down to the bottom of the sea and joined hands in a big circle, dancing slowly round, singing (yes, even under water) in high voices, ending their dance by stamping hard. And as if that was a signal, every fish seemed to wake up and drift lazily upwards, and the big seaweeds rose upwards too, waving as if to say ‘Thankyou’. Two grey seals lifted from the bottom of the sea, and swam over to the elves and nudged them with their noses as if to say 'Thankyou, friends'. The octopus stared at them, then with a cloud of blue-grey ink, it shot away into the deeper water. Slowly all the flashes of colour faded, and you could almost imagine the rainbow had never been broken. Almost.

Lily looked around, and seemed pleased with what had been done. She waved at the elves, turned, then flew from the sea into the river which flowed down from near Dragonmount. She had left several of the elves to carry on tidying the seawater, but now most flew with her. Here in the river, too, the gloom had gone and life was returning. Crayfish raised their claws, little fish stared and flashed away, and all the water plants waved. Lily was soon smiling and clapping to the elves to say ‘Well done. Carry on cleaning’. Then once again she vanished.

The next time she appeared (even if she was a shadow, she was still Lily the Witch) she was high in the sky, sitting on the back of a very large and surprised eagle. The masses of black cloud and the lightning and thunder had faded away. Below, waves on the sea, which had returned to a calm blue, once again splashed quietly on golden sand.

Everywhere in the air there were patches of dirty brown smoke, and muddy looking clouds. The air smelled horribly dirty, and only a few birds could be seen, high in the sky - none close to the ground. She gently hugged the eagle's neck as if to say 'I'm sorry to have to share your journey, my friend, but we must mend the sky' and the eagle turned its head as if to say 'I am happy to help, little mother'. Lily held out her wand, and sang a sad little song as she waved it gently and the eagle flew in great big lazy circles, gradually lower in the air. As they passed, the air cleared, and you could just smell fields below.

There was a shiver down the eagle's back, and a sweet humming in the air behind Lily, and without looking she said 'Your majesty, how are things for your fairies and the plants? Can I really smell wildflowers again?' The Fairy Queen's wings were a blur as she flew alongside the eagle and patted it gently on the head. She turned to Lily. 'It is much hard work', she said. 'Most of the damage has been near Dragonmount, and my fairies have been flying everywhere, talking with their plants and helping them. The little insects which live with the plants were much hurt, and it will take some time for everything to be well again, but yes, the plants are happier and even some of those who were most hurt have been smiling.

The Fairy Queen invited Lily to come and see what had been done. Would you like to join us and see for yourself?' Lily the Witch gave a deep sigh. 'There is still too much to do!', she said. 'But I promise once I have finished cleaning the air I would love to see what you and your fairies have achieved.' She looked down again on the fields, as the clouds slowly turned from brown to white. 'We must work hard and succeed!' she said. And as the Fairy Queen smiled and flew back to the fields below, the elves mind-spoke to her. 'We have found Ludo!' 'Where is he?' she said. 'I am here, witch', came a rough voice. From right behind her, where a black and sparkling figure was flying like Superman.

'Yes, I am here and I am going to end all this right now. Your day is done. I will have my freedom!' said the voice. Lily said nothing, but guided the eagle gently into a curve. 'You cannot face me?' said Ludo. 'What a shame - I would have enjoyed watching your face as your day ended'. He laughed that nasty laugh that the dragons had heard above the mountains. 'But never mind', he said. 'I am generous. I will fry you as you are!' Lily nudged the eagle, and it dropped like a stone, just as a huge flare of energy roasted the place where she'd been flying. 'Now, you elves!' she mind-spoke, and she felt a warmth in her mind as Erzuth mind-spoke her in turn. 'I said we would be with you', she said. And as the elves threw out new dark clouds to hide the sun and stop Ludo from flying, dragon-fire scorched him from behind.

Ludo screamed and flew off to one side. But there was another dragon hidden there, too (you remember, dragons can be very hard to see if they wish, and Erzuth and Rezu had both been hiding in the sky!) and flames met him as he flew away. Again he screamed, and by now Lily the Witch and her eagle were behind him. She took some of her glass bubbles from a pocket, and threw them on his back. They turned into great waves of water as they landed, and with a final scream of rage he fell out of the sky, landing in the river below with an enormous splash and big clouds of steam, which climbed high in the air. The elves who were mending the river climbed all over Ludo, binding him with ropes of wet river weed to stop him flying again.

Once Ludo was still, the elves packed away the dark clouds which had hidden the sun, and the Fairy Queen quickly returned to be with Lily as she stepped from her eagle and gave it a very grateful hug. 'You are indeed the king of the birds', she said, as it climbed into the sky.

The dragons landed on the riverbank as the Fairy Queen and Lily the Witch shared a hug, and then they stood and stared at Ludo – a very wet, scorched, sulky Ludo – as he lay in the river, and the elves waved as if to say 'job done!'

Lily waved in return as they disappeared back into the river water to carry on cleaning. The dragons were really cross. 'Little mother, we cannot free him again after what he has been doing!' they said together. 'No, you're right', she said. 'But we can't send him to prison - no prison would hold him. Yes, I would love to clip his wings and stop him flying, at least then he would not be able to do mischief!' She stood and thought for a very long time. The dragons looked at each other. The Fairy Queen tapped her feet. Even the elves popped up out of the river to see what was happening.

Eventually, she sighed and started emptying her pockets onto the grass. Soon, there was a great big pile of things beside her – bubbles, wands, and lots of other mysterious things which you don't want to know about… 'My goodness', said the Fairy Queen. 'How do your pockets hold so much?' Lily smiled. 'My pockets are as deep as the ocean', she said, 'and they can hold mountains'. And then 'Helloo' came a voice from up the river, and a bundle of fur with a wet nose launched itself into Lily's arms, as Bill and Rags arrived together. She smiled.

'Now', she said. 'Let's decide what to do with that horribly mischievous, tied up bundle', pointing at Ludo as he lay in the water, still and wet. 'We cannot imprison him, little mother.' Rezu said, 'But as you said, if he cannot fly he cannot make mischief. Perhaps if we could clip his wings, that would be ideal. But he doesn't have wings. He just flies like the clouds, and that is what causes problems. How do we stop it? I don't know'. Bill stood looking at the ground. 'It's not just his flying, which is fed by the sun', he said. 'It's what he does while he flies. If he just stopped touching and interfering...' Ah, said Aznath, who had brought the baby dragons with him and joined Rezu and Erzuth on the riverside. 'Yes. That's it, little mother! Let him fly, but stop him changing things. Let him see and smell the things we all love, but not change them. So he can still go to places he loves – like Dragonmount', he said, smiling, 'but then he won't be able to do mischief while he is there. That way he will still feel free.'

The dragons looked at each other. Lily looked at the Fairy Queen. Rags jumped down, and barked. Bill looked up at Lily. There was a long silence. Then Lily nodded her head. The Fairy Queen went and kissed Bill on his cheek, which he touched, looking surprised. Lily looked up at the sky, then at Ludo, then at Aznath. 'My friends, as usual you are right!' She said. She looked through all the things she had unloaded from her pockets, and waved her wand over a tiny, glowing little ball. 'Now', she said. 'Let's turn the elephant into a mouse!'

She went over to Ludo, and popped the little ball into his mouth, then sang a very strange little song. 'That will stop his mischiefs - I hope!' she said. 'Now, I think we can turn him loose', and she waved her little stick over him. He struggled upright, glared at them all, and prepared to fly away. And nobody noticed him spitting out the little ball...

The next morning, Lily woke late – yesterday had been a very busy day – and decided her housework could just wait again. She had a lazy breakfast, then walked down to the little stream that runs past her cottage, to sit in the sun, watch kingfishers, and relax. 'I thought I'd find you here!' said a voice, and Bill walked along Melody Lane to her gate, and sat down with her. And they watched the rainbow antics of the kingfishers. It was a lovely day. High above, unseen, Ludo looked down and plotted his revenge. There would be time.

LILY THE WITCH AND THE FROST KING

It was very early one morning, well before the sun woke up. The birds were still asleep, the bees were in their nests, Lily the Witch was in the middle of a lovely dream, and her elves were snoring in their little hill beside her cottage.

But the Frost King was wide awake. He had been asleep for a very, very long time, deep in the darkest of places – the crystal caves beneath the mountains where dragons lived, but now his old friend Ludo had woken him, and together they were planning to change the world. Things were not as they wanted them to be. The Frost King loved things to be very cold, and Ludo wanted them to be very hot. So they would divide the world between them.

Micky Black

The Frost King left his icy home, spread his wings and flew silently into the dark sky. You could only see him as a blackness moving among the glittering stars. He quickly took control of the night - it became bitterly cold, and icy silver shadows fell everywhere. The woods and their fairy ring wore a white cloak. The little stream outside Lily's cottage was no longer tinkling and gurgling, as a long sheet of ice had covered it. Her orchard became a still, white place where every tree, every branch was dressed in crisp white lace, as frost spread over everything in sight – the trees a silent and ghostly echo against the night sky. Even the grass over the elves' special place, beneath the weeping willow in her garden, turned white like icing on a cake. In her bed, Lily the Witch shivered and pulled the blankets up under her chin, before turning over and grumbling quietly in her sleep.

The Frost King glided silently from corner to corner of the sky, with his arms outstretched and a smile on his face. Not a nice smile. In fact it was very like a cold version of the smile Ludo wore when he was up to mischief, and that wasn't surprising, for Ludo and the Frost King had worked alongside each other many times before. Both of them determined to make the world do what and when they wanted. But not tonight, as tiring of his night's work, but immensely happy, and with the whole world now a beautiful but bitterly cold spider's web of white frost, broken only by little shadows under trees and the dark icy covering of lakes and streams, the Frost King glided silently back to his crystal home among the sleeping hills.

Much later, when the sun rose for dawn, Lily stretched and opened her eyes, before saying hello to her little dog Rags, who normally slept at the foot of her bed, but this morning was curled up beside her. 'My my', she said, 'what a cold night! I hope you could sleep?' and Rags whimpered before giving her a quick 'where's my breakfast?' lick on the chin. It wasn't until she sat up in bed and opened her curtains that Lily realised what had happened, and frowned. She reached for her wand. 'It seems the Frost King is awake', she said.

Once she'd finished breakfast, Lily walked – with her wand firmly gripped in her hand - to the little hill where her elves lived. Rags slipped and slithered around her. The walk wasn't far, but the path was icy, and pretty in its glassiness, and she had to tread carefully. She knocked sharply on the big green door, and it was quickly opened by the Head Elf, who said hello with a worried look on his face. All the elves were waiting to listen to her, and none of them looked very warm.

She told them what she thought may have happened. 'You know of the Frost King' she said. The elves shuffled and looked uneasily at each other. 'I think Ludo may have woken him up. If he is awake, then we shall have to work really quickly to stop our beautiful world being becoming ice then fire. Ludo won't want the ice, but I'm sure they will have some plan...'

The elves muttered to each other, and hissed and stamped their feet (elves always stamp their feet when they get cross). 'I think if he has been woken up, then yes, Ludo will have been behind it, and I suspect they aim to work together so that they can both get what they want. They like very different things and they are both very selfish, and that may give us a chance to stop them. Ludo likes things very hot so he will want to rule the daytime, when the Frost King can't fly, and the Frost King likes them very cold, so he will want to rule the nights, when Ludo can't fly. Probably they will argue. But we must plan now- so be ready!' The elves cheered and clapped, and sang their strange little songs, and Lily smiled.

The Head Elf opened the door, and Lily left their little hill and started walking back to her kitchen, but she had only gone a few paces when she heard a familiar voice. 'Willow', it said. She turned and looked back, and there, sitting under the willow trees which covered the little hill, was a fairy, dressed in a thick white cloak, and carrying a wand with willow tassels at the end. 'Princess Willow!' said Lily. 'What a surprise! How are your trees? How are you?'

The Willow Fairy smiled, before shaking her head and starting to look very sad. 'I am pleased to see you, little mother,' she said. 'But all the fairies are sad today', she said. 'All of us, and all the plants, are much too cold', and she looked up at the willow trees above her. 'I am here to bring you a message from the Fairy Queen, who needs badly to talk with you', and she looked down. Lily smiled. 'Of course', she said. And No sooner had she spoken, than a rainbow appeared in front of her and from it stepped a beautiful little lady, dressed in gold and wearing a beautiful golden crown.

'Your majesty', said Lily. 'Please', said the Fairy Queen, reaching out. 'Little mother, let us talk.' And as she spoke yet another voice joined the conversation. 'Well, bless me', it said, and in from the front garden strode Bill, Lily's best friend. 'May I talk too? I've been sliding everywhere. Why is it so cold? Aaah', and he stopped and bowed. 'Aaah. Your majesty. So, this will be a talking of importance!'

The four of them then greeted each other as old friends, and walked back to Lily's kitchen. 'Well', Lily said. 'Let us all have a Council of War. But before we do, please excuse me while I make some tea. We may as well be comfortable, and sit beside a warm stove!' And so soon, with mugs of tea in their hands, Lily's cats Honey and Marmalade laying on the floor purring, and Rags the little dog wagging his tail, the four friends sat together and looked out of the kitchen window at the orchard, much of which was still sparkling under white frost. But the sun had taken over the sky, and as it shone the frost was quickly disappearing.

'I don't like this' said Bill. 'Everything is going from very cold to very hot too quickly!' 'Yes', said the Fairy Queen. 'You and I will remember the last time this happened, little mother. It is like when the Frost King and Ludo worked together to take over the world'.

'Mmm', said Lily. 'I think they have cooked up a nasty little plan to do that again.' 'Last night when I went to bed, everything seemed as it should be. All the fairies were happy, their plants were healthy, and it was just another warm spring night. And then this morning we must live like polar bears, and by mid-day as sunflowers?' said the Queen. Lily the Witch smiled, grimly, and pointed at the garden. Where the sun shone on the trees, the ice had already melted, and steam was rising into the sky. 'Yes, I well remember the last time, and I think Bill's right', she said. 'We must put a stop to this and quickly. But right now I need time to think. And it's time we may not have…'

There was a tap, tap, tap at the door. Bill went and opened it, and as hot air swept into the room, Lily and the Fairy Queen exchanged glances. Standing at the door was a figure like a small child, all dressed in green. But it wasn't a small child - it was the Head Elf. Hopping up and down, he spoke quickly in a voice which was shaking – 'You know we always use elf magic to see what Ludo's up to. Well, we've lost him, Lily Witch. We can't find him anywhere. We haven't seen him flying away. And there's something wrong with our magic - we can't make things warmer or cooler. They're stuck!'

Everybody stood up and started talking at once. Lily banged the table with her mug and splashed tea everywhere, and they all stopped. ‘I’m sorry your majesty’, she said, and then smiled and looked round at everyone else. ‘But we can’t all be heard at the same time’. She turned to the Head Elf. ‘So, tell us – when did you see he was missing? And what have you done about it?’

Everybody apart from Lily the Witch then sat down. The Head Elf fidgeted from one foot to the other, and said ‘Just after you left us to come back to your cottage, Ludo started to fly. Yes, it was very cold, but the sun was shining as he should. We always watch what the sun’s doing, so we can protect everything. But this time there was a shiver, and the sun started shining brighter and brighter until it got very warm’. ‘We noticed’, said Bill. ‘But where Ludo’s gone we don't know - unless it was underground...' said the Head Elf. 'We've heard sad cries from some of the fairies, so of course we've tried to cool things down - but we can't. Our spells aren’t working. And things just keep getting warmer and warmer’.

And then as if by magic, as the Head Elf finished, a blast of hot air roared through the doorway around him, forcing him to jump and turn at the same time. And then he was staring straight into the glowing face of Ludo himself. A grinning Ludo, with his eyes shining and his dark face crawling with golden sparks. ‘Take a good look at ME’, he sneered at them all. ‘You will have to wait a long, long time for another! Or of course you may cook first’, and he laughed. ‘My friend the sun is now free, and you cannot stop him growing hotter, and hotter, and hotter. And me? ME? I am going where you will never find me, and where I can watch the end of your little world. Any questions?’ And he laughed again. A nasty laugh.

The Head Elf rushed forward to hit him, but everyone jumped to their feet and Lily screamed 'No! No, not on your own. That's what he wants. You would burn to a crisp'. The Head Elf backed away as she turned to Ludo. 'You may think you have been very clever. But you have no plans that we cannot undo. No matter where you go, we shall stop your game.'

She held up her wand. But Ludo just laughed, and in a blaze of energy, he disappeared. Outside, the sky grew brighter and brighter, and the sun, like Ludo, seemed to laugh as he blazed down on them. The four friends stared at each other. The Head Elf looked around, said 'I am so, so sorry' and ran back to the special place. Silence.

The silence lasted for many heartbeats, before everyone slowly sat down again. 'Well', said the Fairy Queen, 'if there was any doubt about what's happening, that must be the end of it.' 'I agree', said Lily the Witch. 'It would have taken us longer to be certain if Ludo hadn't stopped to boast about it. Time is running out, but we must be sure what's happening. Ludo didn't talk about the Frost King, but I'm sure they've planned this together. Cold last night, hot today. Does everyone agree?' they all looked at each other and nodded. Willow, in a quiet voice, said 'My willows are gentle trees, and they are already hurting. And I'm sure all the other plants and their fairies will be hurting too. I agree.'

'We've seen Ludo make trouble many times', said the Fairy Queen. 'But it's been forever since he shared trouble with the Frost King! And if the elves can't make magic, that's really worrying! So for all the fairies, I agree.' 'Yes' said Bill. 'Me too. But how can we stop the sun from burning everything if we can't cool things down?' 'Leave the sun to me and my elves', said Lily. 'I have been thinking, and already have some ideas. Your Majesty, the fairies have very old books hidden away which talk about the Frost King. If we are going to stop this, we need to look at them. Can I please visit your library to see what the books can tell us? Once we find the Frost King, I'm sure we'll find Ludo, too'. The Fairy Queen agreed, they hugged, and agreed Lily the Witch would visit that afternoon. Then a beautiful rainbow appeared in the garden, and Willow and the Fairy Queen walked into it and disappeared.

Lily and Bill looked at each other. 'We need to go and talk with the elves again', she said, and they both crossed the garden – which was now really hot - with Rags the little dog.

The Head Elf let them in, and they all sat down together. 'I am so sorry that I almost touched Ludo all by myself', he said. 'I was shocked and wasn't thinking'. Lily gave him a quick hug. 'You and I have worked together for a very long time', she said. 'I know how brave you are and you've saved me from trouble many times. But when Ludo is blazing hot like that he can be so dangerous. We don't want to lose you - now more than ever we should work together. We must stop the sun cooking everything.' 'But our magic isn't working', said the Head Elf. 'I know', said Lily the Witch. 'It's happened before. But don't worry, I think I have a plan'.

The elves crowded around. 'I think Ludo has put one of his strongest chains on your magic, so that you can't cast spells of your own. Let's see – can you all fly in the air a little, right now, like you usually do?' The elves concentrated and fidgeted, but nothing happened. 'I thought so', said Lily. I think he's left one or more of his golden coins around your little hill – they stop people using magic. We need to find them, now!

Lily, the Head Elf and all the elves rushed out of their little hill and started searching. It didn't take long before the Head Elf shouted 'Here!' and they found not just one but three of Ludo's 'spell stopper' coins. Witches aren't affected by them, so Lily magic'd them gone!

'Now', said Lily the Witch. 'I'm going to talk with my friends the dragons. They can fly as high as the sun and will give me a ride. I will try to throw a net of magic over the sun to send him to sleep. But I shall need your help, so be ready and be quick – I will mind-speak with you, and you will have just moments to act! Once the sun is asleep, I'm sure Ludo will rush to wake him, and I need you to turn the sky dark immediately so that he can't. And if Ludo is working with the Frost King, we shall be closer to catching them both. The Fairy Library will help us too.' The elves cheered and stamped their feet, and Lily waved to them all before leaving and walking back to the cottage with Bill. When they arrived Rags ran out and barked and danced, and they laughed. The sun blazed down from a hot, sulky sky, and Lily couldn't resist a worried glance upwards as they went inside. Then Bill went home after Lily promised to mind-speak him with any news.

She then sat down in a dark, cool corner of her kitchen and listened for Ludo, but she could not 'feel' his presence. Then she thought long and hard about Erzuth, her dragon friend. She had often shared adventures with the big green dragon, and both of them had faced Ludo (far too often, Lily thought). Well, this time they would be out to catch the sun itself… 'Erzuth, my old friend', said Lily, 'please tell me you can hear me'. There was a long pause, then 'Yes, little mother', came a rumbling voice. 'This is a pleasure…' 'Erm, no, it's work', said Lily, and she explained what had happened, and what she hoped to do about it. 'Everybody needs your help'. 'My goodness', said Erzuth. 'Of course I will help. What an adventure – two old friends out to catch the sun itself!' And so they agreed to meet on the green beside the little stream, after Lily had visited the Fairy Library.

Once the day was done, and the sun had gone to bed, the Frost King laughed out loud to himself as he flew slowly over the darkness below, bringing bitter cold everywhere. Icicles formed around windows and doorways, and coated hills and valleys, woods and streams, roadsides and orchards with glistening ice. To go for a walk was to risk being frozen, or at best slipping and sliding all over everywhere. Then it began to snow, lightly at first and then more and more heavily, until the whole world was white. 'And still tomorrow everything will again be roasting hot, and my brother and I will have all we need, everything we want', he thought to himself as he flew one more time over the Fairy Ring, before turning silently in the sky and returning to his crystal hide-away.

Once again Lily the Witch shivered in her sleep, with her little dog Rags and the two cats laying beside her in an effort to keep warm. Rags whimpered, and Lily groaned gently, before sitting up with a start and opening her curtains. The whole world wore white, and in between black snow clouds the stars shone viciously from a black sky. She muttered under her breath and looked at her clock. It was four o'clock in the morning. 'At least', she said to herself, 'he isn't sitting outside my window laughing at me!' Then she slipped back under her covers and tried to sleep, A deep voice murmured in her mind 'It is just as cold here, little mother. But we shall soon put everything right', and the image of a smiling dragon stayed in her mind as she drifted back into an uncomfortable sleep.

Soon enough, it was morning. Frost had invaded even the insides of the windows, and to breathe was to steam. Lily climbed shivering and bleary out of bed, scattering her furry friends all over the floor, and wrapped herself in the thick blanket which covered her bed, then went as quickly as she could downstairs to the kitchen, where she laid the biggest fire she could and put on the kettle, before feeding her animals, which were all shivering around her feet. Soon enough, the room began to warm. 'Not too soon', she muttered to herself, getting dressed as closely to the fire as possible. She poked her head out of the back door to see what the world outside was doing. Snow was everywhere, but as the sun rose in the sky, it began steaming, and the trees in her orchard released great clumps of snow before showing their bare black arms to the sky. 'My poor orchard', she said. 'We shall do our best today to end this mischief, I just hope you don't suffer too much, and your fruit is safe!'

The morning quickly heated up and soon all the ice and snow had gone. All the trees and plants and their fairies groaned as the sun grew hotter and hotter. 'Be strong, my children', said the Fairy Queen. 'Trust the little mother'. Yet again, in the back of her mind she heard mocking, nasty laughter.

Once she was warm and dressed, and her animals had been fed, Lily the Witch walked carefully over to the elves' little hill. By this time the sun, barely over the horizon, was already warm on her shoulders, and she frowned. 'We shall see, my friend, we shall see who is smiling last. We shall see, Ludo'. The snow was fast disappearing as she knocked on the big green door, and as it opened she was immediately surrounded by anxious and cold-looking elves. 'Today we shall see, my friends', she said, before sitting down with them all to talk through her plan.

'This morning I shall visit the Fairy Queen, and the Fairy Library, and explore the story of the Frost King.' she said. 'He and his brother Ludo have been far too busy for their own good - or for ours'. The elves nodded. 'Once I have his secrets we shall find both of them. But before we find the Frost King, we must make the sun behave – he is freed, and will keep burning hotter and hotter. So our friend Erzuth the dragon and I will pay him a little visit later this morning. Remember - be ready to blacken the sky!

Soon afterwards, she made her way to the Fairy Ring in the woods, with Rags dancing around her feet. The Fairy Queen was sitting beside the lake, talking with Willow, when Lily arrived. They waved at each other and both the Queen and Willow stood. 'Another blissfully warm night and now a cold day', joked Lily. 'Can we spend some time with your old stories?' 'Follow me, little mother', said the Queen, and walked into the lake. Lily followed, picking up Rags. 'Do we have to get wet first?' she said. 'No' said Willow, 'this is no ordinary lake. It has been the heart of the Fairy Kingdom for ever. Just trust the fairies', and she followed the Queen into the water. Shrugging her shoulders, and holding tight to Rags, Lily the Witch followed. She felt very strange, as the water refused to touch her, and she was able to walk deeper and deeper without getting at all wet. Rags was fascinated, as little fish came to see who was walking through their space, but when he put out a paw the water receded around it, and the little fish vanished.

Then they came to an old doorway and through it into a dry open space with shelves and shelves of books, all lit as though by daylight. The Fairy Library. The Queen walked straight to a shelf stacked with very dirty-looking and dusty books. 'We are lucky', she said. 'Neither time nor insects can do any damage here. Now - these are the books which recorded our adventures years ago with the

Frost King', and she lifted down three tired-looking books. 'Are they going to survive being opened?' said Lily. 'Oh yes', said the Fairy Queen, and she wiped her hand across the covers of the books one by one. Quickly, the books changed, and looked as though they were new. Lily the Witch spent a long time reading through them before rubbing her forehead and saying 'Mmm, I did wonder. The Frost King is in the crystal caves under Dragonmount! Which means Ludo must be nearby. But they cannot stay there. It is not where they belong!'

Lily turned to the Fairy Queen. 'A million thanks, your majesty', she said. 'Now I must fly – really fly, I have asked my old dragon friend Erzuth to help me dim the sun today, and that will make it cooler, and bring some relief to everyone!' The Queen smiled. 'And Ludo, and his brother the Frost King?' she said. 'Thanks to the Fairy Library', said Lily, 'I think I know where to look, and I hope there will be a quick finish to this business', and she followed the Queen back through the door and through the water, with Rags held tight in her arms. The little fish crowded around again as if to say 'Goodbye, and good luck', and moments later they were walking out of the water, as dry as when they arrived. But now there were hundreds of fairies standing around the lake, waiting to see them, and when Lily the Witch explained what she hoped to do, they stood up and sang a very sweet, short song. 'They are wishing you luck, in the Fairy way', said the Queen, before she embraced Lily. There was a shimmering over the lake and a rainbow appeared. 'Just walk onto it as though it was a path', said the Queen. 'You will be home in seconds'. And she was.

As Lily stepped off at her cottage, the rainbow faded and disappeared, and she stood still for a moment in her garden, thinking hard then using mind-speak. 'Erzuth, my friend, we have some good news and now our game should begin – I will explain as we go'. Quickly, a very rumbly voice replied 'Yes, I am ready, little mother, and I shall fly to meet you as we arranged'. Lily went inside the cottage and put Rags down next to Honey and Marmalade, saying 'I need you to look after our home, I must fly with Erzuth!' and then she went her bedroom to collect some strange things – not least a rolled-up net which seemed to glow and sparkle in her arms. A surprise awaited her in the kitchen – Bill had returned and was busily making some tea.

They smiled at each other, and he said 'I overheard you mind-speaking with Erzuth, and came at once. I expect you will say you don't have time for tea, but I wouldn't be anywhere else while your cottage is empty, and I will wait with my tea, and maybe with some of your apple pie?' and Lily nodded and smiled. Just as a huge shadow spread over the cottage, and there was a rustling of wings as Erzuth carefully landed on the little green beside the stream. 'I am here, little mother', she mind-spoke. Lily waved at her friends through the heat of the day, and then to the elves, who had opened their door to watch, and climbed carefully onto Erzuth's back. 'Let's go!', she said.

They flew high and fast. Soon the sky was dark blue and the air was cooler, and looking down Mother Milo could see her cottage quickly getting smaller as they climbed the air. 'My friend' she said, 'we need to get as close to the sun as we can, so that I can throw this net over him. I hope he will think this just a visit by a curious dragon, and not take too much notice, but we shall see…' 'Indeed', rumbled Erzuth. 'I will do my best to be a curious dragon', and she mind-spoke a picture of smiling dragon faces to Lily. Soon, the sun was getting large, and Erzuth flew in great loops and whirls around him. 'Ready?' she said. 'Yes', said Lily the Witch. 'Then now we go', said Erzuth, and went even closer to the sun. The heat was immense, but Lily leaned around Erzuth's neck, and carefully threw her net.

Immediately the sky darkened. There was a squeal of shock from the sun as he was covered, and the net began to smoke at the edges. 'Now!' mind-spoke Lily to the elves, and there was a whisper in the air as they magicked fierce blackness across the sky. Thunder rumbled and a hot wind blew. 'Quick', said Lily. 'We don't want to be fried by lightning!' 'Don't worry', said Erzuth. 'Just hold tight', and she dropped like a stone and flew along the little stream beside the cottage. 'Now', she said, 'do you have a plan for dealing with the brothers?'

'Yes', said Lily. 'The Fairy Library is wonderful. The old stories showed me the crystal caves near your home. You cannot mind-read inside them, and the brothers can laugh in secret there about what they have done. They will think they are safe, and they definitely won't care about our world, only their greed. My plan is to go to Dragonmount, and once they realise the heat is turned off Ludo will want to investigate - but he won't know we're waiting for him or that he cannot fly'. 'Then I must warn Rezu', said Erzuth. 'She can keep her children safe, then surprise him and keep him busy until we arrive. I will fly as fast as I can', and she flew faster and faster until the ground below was a blur.

In the distance, the sharp peak of Dragonmount was looming larger and larger. A huge dragon could be seen flying high in the air, around the top of the mountain. Rezu! And with her were three small shapes, the young dragons. 'Erzuth, my friend', said Lily the Witch, 'I thought Rezu would keep her children in a safe place?' 'Little mother', said Erzuth, 'they are young dragons. Like all young things they are very brave. They will fly away if they have to - and Rezu is there. She will look after them'.

Erzuth was getting very close to Dragonmount now, and as they watched all the dragons seemed to fade from the sky 'they have decided not to be seen', said Erzuth. Both she and Lily watched everywhere for Ludo. Then he appeared, on foot, from around the other side of Dragonmount. A sheet of flame washed over him ('That's Rezu', said Erzuth) and he dropped onto the mountain before trying again to stagger into the sky, but the sun had been darkened by the elves' magic, and he couldn't. Erzuth and Lily arrived just as he was trying again to leap into the air, but when he saw two dragons he hesitated, and that gave Lily just enough time to take several small glassy balls from her pocket, and threw them into the air above him. As they fell, they drenched him in a huge stream of water. He screamed and stopped moving, but called out 'Brother, help me!' and as he did so the water turned to ice, for there, clambering out of a mountain cave, was the Frost King himself!

The Frost King did not like being woken up during the day. It was warm and bright, and he liked it cold and dark. What was worse, he couldn't fly in daylight, only at night. And he had been deeply asleep. During the night he had been very busy flying the sky, and making things cold, and he was very tired. But now he had been woken by his brother Ludo, and those horrible flying things that breathed fire were glaring at him from the sky. Now he wasn't just angry – he was furious. He spread cold as far as he could, and the ice spread wider and wider, except around his brother, but he couldn't climb into the air to face these monsters, and the two dragons were weaving special patterns around the two of them. Patterns which were sending them both to sleep. He struggled, and slithered closer to Ludo, but he had to keep his distance because although Ludo couldn't move, he too was furious, and so very very hot!

The air between the brothers shimmered, then there was a bang and a flash from the larger of the two flying dragons, and it was then that the Frost King noticed a human sitting on its back, waving a wand. The moment lasted longer and longer, and as if in slow motion, the flash spread around him and his brother Ludo like a wall of golden light, until very quickly neither of them could move at all. The last thing the Frost King did before he was forced to sleep was to scream 'Lily Witch!' then he lay still. Once the brothers had stopped moving, Erzuth and Rezu landed beside them, and Lily climbed down.

'Thankyou my friends', she said. 'Now we must hurry - they won't stay like this for long, and we need to make the world safe once more!' 'What can you do, little mother? They are really really powerful, the two of them, and one is burning hot and the other freezing cold.' said Rezu. 'I could not lift either of them!' 'Well, we cannot just put the Frost King back in that crystal cave', said Lily the Witch. 'Just like Ludo, the Frost King must go back to his true home'. The two dragons looked at each other, and then back at her, ready to throw questions. 'No, not now. We must act - questions later' she said. 'Neither of them really belongs in our world, and your beautiful crystal caves certainly deserve far better company! I must send them both into space. Ludo belongs on one side of the Moon where the sun always shines, and the Frost King on the other where it is always dark and bitterly cold. My magic will help send them, but I cannot do it alone, and you big dragons cannot help. No, I need what only your children can give, because all children dream magic!'

The little dragons peeped around large rocks, where they had been hiding.'Yes, little mother?' they said together. Lily explained. I can weave spells around both of them, but I need you three little dragons to make a wish. Your wishes nearly always come true!' (Erzuth and Rezu smiled and nodded). The wish is that they go home. That's all. Just wish them home'. The three little dragons - two green, one red and gold - smiled too. 'Right', said Lily, and she knelt on the grass and with her wand wove magical patterns. And soon the moon appeared - not in the sky, but small, in the air in front of them. The brothers snored and stayed bound.

'Now', said Lily the Witch, and the little dragons closed their eyes and concentrated. And within a heartbeat, Ludo and the Frost King floated into the air, The moon floated away in front of them and the brothers followed, and they all rose faster and faster into the sky. It was silent, and then from far away and high above they heard angry shouts as the brothers woke and realised what was happening.

The big dragons smiled (have you ever seen a dragon smile?) and the little dragons peeped out of the corner of their eyes, as the moon flew ever higher back into the sky. Lily the Witch stood still for a very long time looking at the moon as it shone peacefully over everything. The little dragons sat around, looking up with astonishment at what they had helped achieve. Erzuth rumbled in their minds. ‘It is done, little mother. They may dream but their dreams can only heat and freeze the moon, leaving our world alone. Now hold my scales – they will warm you’. And they all - Erzuth, Rezu, the little dragons and Lily the Witch - flew quietly and quickly down through the gathering twilight to the little green near the cottage. Lily thanked them all. ‘What a day’ she said. ‘It was’, rumbled Rezu as she climbed down. 'Now - will the brothers stay on the moon, little mother?' 'I hope so. That was a great big magic which we had to do together', Lily said. 'so I think they will stay there at least until there is another eclipse'.

'What is an eclipse?' chorused the little dragons. 'Ah', said Lily. 'Your mother will tell you all about it. That's when the moon and the sun and our world hide from each other. I just hope that they can't slide back to us then. Now - a great big thankyou, and sleep well', and the dragons flew lazily away into the night sky, rumbling 'Good night, little mother. Sleep warmly, sleep well!' Lily smiled and sent a big hug.

When Lily the Witch entered her kitchen, there was a chorus of loud snores. Bill was sprawled across her favourite armchair, with several empty teacups by his side and with Honey on his lap, Marmalade was curled up near to the fireplace. Lily looked around and smiled, before coughing gently into her hand. Nothing happened – everyone slept on. She tried again, a little louder, and Honey's ears pricked up, while Rags rolled over, right way up, and opened an eye. Then the noise started – Bill started to yawn, looked around, and said 'My, my'. Honey jumped off his lap, narrowly missing the teacups, and leaped into Lily's arms. Marmalade woke and stretched. Then to a chorus of woofs, miaows and 'My my's', the room woke up.

Lily made some fresh tea as she described what had been happening. 'Thankyou all for looking after my little cottage', she said. I have had a very busy day, and a very good one. We have sent both those rascals back where they belong'. 'Good', said Bill. 'Where was that?' and when Lily said 'the Moon!' he nearly fell over backwards. 'I'll explain later', she said. 'Now I must go and tell the elves, and the Fairy Queen'. No sooner had she said 'Fairy Queen' than a familiar rainbow appeared beside the cottage door, and the Queen and Willow stood there, their eyes shining and big smiles on their faces.

'Well', said Lily, smiling in return - 'why don't we all go and see the elves!

The Fairy Queen and Willow followed Lily to the elves' little hill. She knocked on the big green door, but there was no reply. She frowned and knocked again, and there was still no reply, so she opened the door. To her amazement, the elves' home was empty! There wasn't a single elf to be seen! She turned to sound the alarm and run back to her cottage, and then sat down with a bump. There, behind her, grinning, were not only the Fairy Queen and Willow, but her elves and a whole host of fairies. 'How…' she said.

The Fairy Queen stepped forward. 'Fairy magic', she said. You walked right past them on your way here but you couldn't see or hear them! We all wanted to welcome you back and to thank you. The world is a much calmer place! I have been watching what you did, and we can never thank you enough. It was the elves' idea to empty the special place, and we couldn't say no. And we also wanted to thank your friends' - and the mist completely cleared to reveal Erzuth, Rezu and the baby dragons. 'My, what a surprise', said Lily, recovering her smile. 'I don't know what to say'. 'Say nothing', said Bill, emerging from the kitchen with a tray full of teacups, and Rags, Honey, and Marmalade. 'We are all your friends and friends do not need words'.

The evening was warm, and the moon shone brightly (Lily the Witch looked up several times but nothing odd could be seen), and the friends spent many a long while laughing and talking before sleepiness brought the day to a comfortable end, Bill was magicked home by the Fairy Queen, the dragons all flew back to Dragonmount, the fairies returned to the Fairy Ring, and Lily and her pets went to bed, promising that they would all meet again soon. And they did.